A Candlelight Ecstasy Romance ™

"COME HERE, SWEET LADY. . . ."

He bent his head to kiss the soft, white flesh at the base of her throat, and then his mouth fastened upon hers once more.

She gasped as unfamiliar sensations spread like fire through her body. How she wanted to respond to him! Yet darkness in the form of terror overcame her. Even as a young girl she had sworn that she would be beholden to no one. She would not be vulnerable. She would not be the fool! With a muffled sob she tore herself away.

"Bobbie, what's the matter?" he asked, his eyes betraying his surprise.

"Nothing. Just leave me alone," she whispered and turned to run away. . . .

CANDLELIGHT ECSTASY ROMANCES™

CHAMPAGNE AND RED ROSES

Sheila Paulos

A CANDLELIGHT ECSTASY ROMANCE™

Published by
Dell Publishing Co., Inc.
1 Dag Hammarskjold Plaza
New York, New York 10017

Dell ® TM 681510, Dell Publishing Co., Inc.
Candlelight Ecstasy Romance™ is a trademark of
Dell Publishing Co., Inc.,
New York, New York.

ISBN: 0-440-11262-1

Printed in the United States of America

First printing—August 1982

Dear Reader:

In response to your continued enthusiasm for Candlelight Ecstasy Romances™, we are increasing the number of new titles from four to six per month.

We are delighted to present sensuous novels set in America, depicting modern American men and women as they confront the provocative problems of modern relationships.

Throughout the history of the Candlelight line, Dell has tried to maintain a high standard of excellence, to give you the finest in reading enjoyment. That is now and will remain our most ardent ambition.

Anne Gisonny
Editor
Candlelight Romances

CHAPTER I

Bobbie put down her pencil and a triumphant smile spread slowly over her well-scrubbed face, lighting up her gray eyes. Her gaze remained riveted to the drawing board. This cartoon was a winner and it was going to wow all those doubting Thomases at the newspaper who were waiting for her to fail and lose her job. Then they could smugly say to each other that equality between the sexes was fine but . . . The next cartoonist would surely be a balding, gruff-voiced man of experience who would stay on the job forever. Bobbie sighed, banishing the dark thoughts from her mind. Her job was a plum and she was going to keep it. The cartoon in front of her was proof of that.

No sooner had she walked into the office this morning, poured herself a cup of black coffee, and sat down at her wide metal desk than a messenger ran over to tell her the chief was waiting to talk to her in his office.

Not a man to mince words, the chief, editor-in-chief of the *Milwaukee Post,* one of the leading newspapers in Wisconsin, had nodded at her in greeting. Cal Nesbitt looked every bit the part he was playing. The sleeves of his open-necked white shirt were rolled up; his tie was stuck in a back pocket (Bobbie guessed that he actually wore it around his neck a total of ten minutes a day); his face, even at nine o'clock in the morning, sported a five-o'clock shadow; and his eyes were bloodshot (whether from drink, worry, or lack of sleep Bobbie had not yet ascertained).

"Get the mayor!" he said and then waved her away.

"And good luck, you'll need it," she heard him say as she closed the door behind her.

Talk about the social amenities, she thought as she hurried back to her desk. He certainly wasn't going to win any popularity contests. At any rate she knew what her assignment was. She had six hours before deadline and before she knew what her fate in the profession was to be. She couldn't muff her first assignment, and she didn't.

The floor around her was strewn with papers from her overflowing wastepaper basket. Finally she had come up with a workable idea—with a half hour to spare. She drew a knight in shining armor slaying a dragon in order to save a beautiful damsel in distress. The knight was Mayor Allen. The armor and white horse represented his conservative fiscal policies. The dragon was a huddled mass of poor women lying in the rubble of their day-care center. And the beautiful damsel was clothed in diamonds and fur and was distressed at the loss of her tax dollars. She had sketched the cartoon skillfully, yet with a touch of humor. The mayor's teeth gleamed in the light, and his silver-flecked hair shone like a crown. He looked like a prince errant, and Bobbie knew that he often acted like one.

Bobbie, like her newspaper, was a dyed-in-the-wool liberal. The mayor, youngish, handsome, dashing, and as charming as they come, could be no more conservative. The *Post* wanted to do him in and nothing could gladden Bobbie's heart more than to help. Being the kind of person who would give away her last dime to one needier than herself, she was troubled by the conservative tide washing over the country. She felt terribly lucky to have landed this job as cartoonist for the *Post* for she could work according to her conscience and yet fulfill herself artistically.

Bobbie hadn't always been so fortunate. After having worked her way through art school, she had held a variety of jobs: drawing illustrations for clothing sales, doing an occasional poster for almost no fee, painting signs. And then a month ago, on the day of her twenty-seventh birthday, she had heard about this opening at the *Post*. Though she hadn't really thought she'd get the job, since the competition was stiff, she knew she owed it to herself to apply. She had gathered a small portfolio together, brazened her way into the Chief's office, talked a blue streak, and sat in openmouthed shock as she heard the taciturn Nesbitt admit that the paper suffered from tired blood and he thought he'd take a chance with a fresh talent. She had six weeks to prove herself, and if she didn't make it, for this was not a union job, she'd be out pounding the pavements again and free-lancing. The first month had been spent in observation under the tutelage of her departing predecessor, and these next two weeks were going to see her career well started or would see her as a flash in the pan.

Newspaper people, she had always thought, were nice, caring types. To her dismay, she found the same sort of pettiness and office politics that one would find among the salespeople in a dime store. Here it was just disguised a little better.

Hermani Dabo, the gossip columnist, who wore too much makeup to hide the remorseless signs of aging, resented Bobbie's cover-girl complexion and her ingenuous smile; some of the city reporters resented an inexperienced outsider stepping in to fill so important a position when they had to climb the ladder, starting at copy boy or mail clerk. They thought her gender had gained her privilege that they had fought to attain. Perhaps they were right. But Bobbie was disinclined to argue with Lady Luck. Let

9

them dislike her. She had her job and she had her talent and her wit to keep it.

Bobbie brushed her pale blond hair carelessly back so it wouldn't fall over her glasses. The color of her hair against the natural ivory of her cheeks lent her a delicate appearance. Some, if they didn't like her, would say she looked washed out, faded. Bobbie, the despair of a vain mother, tuned out all beauty hints. She didn't care to look beautiful. All she wanted was to be successful. Her sister was the beautiful one, and Bobbie knew she could never look like that. So why pretend to be what you couldn't be? What she did have, she knew, was a good head on her shoulders and determination. Even as a young child she had known she would make something of herself.

She held up the cartoon to the light. The lines were bold, drawn with a strong hand. The conception was clever and biting. This would do. She ripped it carefully out of her large drawing pad and walked with it to Nesbitt's office. She knocked and with a heartbeat that was only a shade faster than normal walked in with head held high.

"Here it is." She held out her work.

Nesbitt took it from her and, holding it in front of him, sat back in his cracked leather swivel chair. Bobbie's nervousness increased as she stood in front of him, like an abashed fourth-grader, shifting from one foot to the other. He didn't say anything for what seemed like an eternity, though it couldn't have been more than three minutes. When finally he looked up, Nesbitt leveled a steady gaze at her and barked, "I like it. It'll hit the stands in the late edition.

"The mayor's giving a press conference at City Hall at four thirty. Cover it. Maybe you'll get some inspiration for a follow-up for tomorrow's paper. And if we can nail him on this day-care issue, we'll get public support and maybe we'll get the bum out of office. Good work."

10

Bobbie nearly skipped out of the office, sure she could be no happier had she been awarded the Pulitzer prize. He liked it. Good work, he said. Bobbie didn't even know she was grinning from ear to ear till she heard Hermani ask if she had taken happy pills with her lunch. Her grin quickly turned to a glower as she shook her head. Hermani would do anything to spoil someone's day.

Bobbie glanced at her wrist. Three o'clock. She had some time for a coffee break before the conference at City Hall. And by that time the papers would be off the presses and she would see her first signed cartoon actually in print! If she weren't in a place of business surrounded by sophisticates, she would do handstands. Her cartoon, her very own baby, for all the world to see! And if her luck held out, they would notice it at City Hall and think of her as a force to be reckoned with! Yes, her! Little Bobbie Schaeffer from 77th Street and Burleigh.

She took another cup of coffee, her fourth of the day, and, holding it in one hand, leaned all the way back in her chair, tipping it back against the wall so she could stretch her legs out and rest her feet on her desk. Why not bask in her success, for say twenty minutes? she thought. As she took the last sip of her coffee, a tasty brew for so late in the day, she put on her pea jacket and knotted her barberry-colored scarf against the blustery winds of early spring. She made sure to pick up a copy of the paper and after a discreet peek at the editorial page tucked it under her arm and headed for her car and the short trip to City Hall. She parked her car in the lot behind the imposing structure and hurried through the main doors just behind a small group of reporters. As she made ready to follow them, for they looked as though they knew where they were heading, she was accosted by a guard in a black uniform with two shining rows of brass buttons.

"Closed to the public, ma'am. Sorry." He made ready to usher her out.

"I'm not the public. I mean"—she blushed—"I'm the press."

"Your pass, please," he said noncommittally, though she read disbelief in his eyes.

"Of course." She riffled through her purse till she came up with the laminated card sporting her picture.

The guard studied it.

"You from a student paper?" he asked.

"The *Milwaukee Post,*" she replied somewhat stiffly as she brushed past him, eager not to miss anything important. That some women might consider it a compliment to be thought ten years their junior had never occurred to Bobbie. Her youthful appearance was a hindrance to her, yet not so much so, that she cared to cultivate a more mature appearance.

The press gallery was filled, though the mayor was not due for another ten minutes. With a sinking heart Bobbie searched the crowded room for a seat. The only one available, it seemed, was right next to Hermani. Knowing Hermani with her sharp tongue and sharper pen, it was easy to figure why people shied away from her. Bobbie made her way to the chair, determined to smile sweetly and grow a thick skin.

"Are you saving this for anyone?" she asked.

"I wish I were," Hermani grumbled as she removed her coat from the seat. Hardly had Bobbie settled herself down when she felt an expectant hush fall over the room. An unwitting gasp escaped her as she watched Mayor Allen stride to the front of the crowded room. This was the first time she had seen him in person, and though she was aware from pictures and television that he was good-looking, she had not known how devastatingly handsome he was. Though none of Milwaukee's previous mayors had

12

engendered such media interest, Dan Allen never failed to pack a press room. He exuded a feeling of power and charisma combined with a sharp intelligence that gave people the sense of seeing history unfold. For some strange reason his dark, masterful looks did not photograph well. He was a big man—Bobbie guessed him to be at least six one—and the powerful muscles of his back and shoulders rippled as he moved, even through the Savile Row cut of his silk suit. He was the kind of man, Bobbie guessed, who could reduce even the coolest denizens of the night to wobbly-kneed gigglers. Her cartoonist's conception of him had not been off target, then.

Hermani eyed her slyly. "He is—what do they say?—a hunk, *n'est-ce pas?*"

Bobbie didn't deign to answer. She couldn't tear her eyes from the mayor had she wanted to anyway.

"Ladies and gentlemen, welcome, and I am at your mercy," he announced in his deep, rich voice, with a rakish smile.

Hands flew up and waved wildly as reporters vied with each other for the opportunity to ask the question that they had worked half a day perfecting. Television cameras whirred and flash bulbs clicked, and the atmosphere that before had been one of ordinary excitement now became charged with his presence. Having come to observe and not to participate, Bobbie was one of the few whose hands remained down.

"What's your new policy on rent control?"

"How do you reconcile your stand on the firemen's strike with your view about government laissez-faire?"

"What are you going to do about the water shortage?"

"Are you working to get additional federal funding for the city?"

The questions went on and on, fired at him in the staccato voices of ardent reporters. The din was deafening as

13

each reporter finished and the others leaped to their feet and cried in unison, "Mr. Mayor!"

Bobbie was impressed that he knew each reporter's name as he called on them, or perhaps, she thought later, he only called on the ones whose names he knew. His answers were terse and to the point. She liked the fact that he didn't skirt issues, and on the one occasion when he didn't know an answer, he admitted it and promised to look into the matter. She hated his politics but she admired, she grudgingly admitted to herself, the way he handled himself with this hostile group of reporters. Always polite, always informed, he was undoubtedly a professional. Almost without realizing it Bobbie felt her hand go up.

"You." He pointed. "The young lady in blue. What's your name first?" He was smiling. Was it her name he was asking? She was momentarily confused.

"Bobbie Schaeffer, Mr. Mayor." She thought she saw a flicker of recognition in his eyes before the mask went up.

"Isn't it fiscally unsound to close the city day-care centers? Working mothers who are contributing tax dollars to the city coffers will only end up on its welfare rolls."

"We have a city government to run, not a nursery school. Anyone who wants to work will find a way. Next question."

Bobbie fumed in her seat. What a cold, infuriating, unfeeling man! she thought as the mayor picked another reporter. The questioner was her next-door neighbor, Hermani.

"And how," she intoned in her saccharine Hungarian accent, "does the mayor like his eggs?" Everyone laughed.

"In the morning," came the reply. He turned from the podium that had been brought in front of him. As he left the room his eyes caught Bobby's and locked with hers for no more than a split second. In that time her universe

14

seemed to explode, and nothing existed except those eyes, big, clear, and shining emeralds. He was gone. Everyone was moving. Bobbie rose to find herself the last one in the room. She hurried home.

CHAPTER II

Bobbie groaned. Though she lay curled snugly in her big down quilt, her muscles aching from her long day, sleep eluded her. And when finally it did come, it was a dizzying half sleep. Even semiconscious she was puzzled at the face, disturbingly like the mayor's, that faded in and out of her dreams. The alarm rang just as she was entering that state of deep restfulness that she so sorely needed. Sitting up reluctantly, she rubbed her eyes and pulled her mouth into a grimace as she recalled the cause of her insomnia. She could behave like a star-struck teen-ager at times. She pulled on her old terry-cloth bathrobe, shuffled into the kitchen, and poured herself a full ten-ounce glass of orange juice. She opened the door for the morning paper, then sat down for her daily dose of vitamin C and news. Even before she scanned the headlines, she opened to Ann Landers's column. She was positively addicted to it and hoped that no one would ever find out. It was only after she pondered Ann's solution to the in-law problems or the neighbor problems that she felt wide awake. She wondered if other people had as much fun with the advice columns as she did, and if they too wrote imaginary letters and answers while standing in line at the supermarket or sitting on a bus.

The front page of the paper was full of what you'd expect: catastrophes, scandals, and taxes. It was page two that plunged her into a dither. There was Mayor Allen's photograph. His smile was brazen, insolent even, exactly as the smile in her dreams. The account of his press conference of the previous evening portrayed him exactly as he was—a selfish, opportunistic politician. Her contempt for his opinions was renewed as she reviewed his words, then with vigor she gave herself to the problem of another cartoon.

She removed herself from the kitchen alcove and sat on her white tuxedo sofa facing glass patio doors that looked out on the lake, as was her custom, to ponder some ideas for her day's work. She did this whether it was a For Sale sign she was about to design or, as today, an important cartoon.

The superb lake view was one of the things that attracted her to this apartment in a renovated town house, although she liked the Victorian wood moldings on the walls and the big bay windows. A year ago when she had moved in here she had had to stretch her budget to afford it, but she was glad of it. It was a special apartment and she was a special girl, so the two of them deserved each other, she had thought, rationalizing the rent to herself. Anyway, what was so good about eating steak?

She turned over the mayor's words in her mind. Her inclination was to do another cartoon on the subject of the closed day-care center. It was a good issue, for few people could feign indifference to the plight of poor children. But she needed a new angle, something clever and biting. Her mind wandered. Unable to concentrate, she got up to satisfy the stirrings of a faint hunger. Though she knew it was unsound nutrition, she tended to avoid breakfast. But with her lack of sleep she decided she ought to at least have some protein to keep her going.

As she broke two eggs into the pan she thought about the mayor's answer to Hermani's question. He liked his

17

eggs in the morning, he'd said. An inspiration lit up her eyes. Of course! Great idea! She could show the mayor sitting down to a mound of eggs, one hand salting his eggs with a shaker in the form of a broken-down woman labeled Indifference to the Poor, the other hand holding a smiling pepper shaker labeled Charm.

Whenever she got an idea, the adrenaline started pumping, and today was no exception. She turned the eggs onto a plate, then ran into the bathroom, splashed water on her face, ran a brush through her hair, and threw on a gray and white striped wraparound skirt and a gray tailored shirt. Forgetting to water her limp-looking plants, or to eat her eggs, she dashed out the door and drove to work, weaving rapidly in and out of traffic. Barely aware of the drivers honking at her and shouting imprecations, she got to the office in record time, fetched coffee, and sat down to some serious drawing.

It was only about twenty drafts and three hours later that she came up with a version that satisfied her exacting eye. She giggled to herself. She was doing it—succeeding in a tough field—and she would do it again and again. As she had done yesterday, she tore out the sheet from her drawing pad, knocked on the chief's door, and handed him the drawing. The only difference was that today her heart rate was perfectly normal and her palms were dry.

"Good work." He paused. "Take the rest of the day off, but *don't* get used to half days."

"Thank you," she said, smiling happily.

Back at her desk she pondered the alternatives for the afternoon. Shopping was out. She was not a shopper. She didn't like seeing movies during the day. Her friends were busy either with jobs or babies. She knew what to do! She'd go to the zoo! The Milwaukee Zoo was one of her favorite places. The animals always seemed happy and energetic and clean. But first she intended to do a little research on the mayor. If breaking his grip on the power structure of this city was her project, she needed to arm herself with a lot more knowledge. She headed for the stacks. Mike, the assistant in charge, got her microfilm for the last two years, and before she knew it, she was elbow deep in news of the mayoralty campaign, feature stories about His Honor, and personality profiles. The more she read, the more she disliked him. He was, by all accounts, too arrogant, too handsome, and too rich for her blood. Men like that ought to be sailing yachts, not running a city. She ignored the fact that he appeared extremely capable, for her feelings toward him were of visceral dislike. His only redeeming quality, as far as she could tell, was that he loved to play the piano and listened to Schubert symphonies to relax. Two o'clock flew by, then three, then four, and Mike was telling her he had to put the microfilm away. So much for the zoo, she thought ruefully.

At home that evening, she made herself a spinach quiche, poured a glass of Burgundy, and dined to a panorama of the setting sun. Tired and content, she fell asleep at nine o'clock to the sound of country-western on her clock radio.

The next morning Bobbie awoke, thankfully refreshed, to a day sweet with the sounds and smells of spring. She chose her clothes with care, not in the mood for some reason to look drab today. She didn't have many fashionable things but the Diane Von Furstenberg shirtwaist dress in mauve and deep purple was one of them. She drove with more courtesy than usual, said a cheery hello to everyone she met on the way to her desk, even Hermani. There were probably especially good ions in the air today, she thought.

As she approached her cubicle she stopped. There was a huge bouquet of red roses on her desk. Now who would ever do that? she asked herself in wonderment. She got the answer when she opened a little card stuck between the delicate blossoms.

Roses are red.
Violets are blue.
I'm the mayor.
Who the devil are you?
I'll have my car pick you up at five for dinner.

Bobbie was amused despite herself. The mayor was a character and a presumptuous one at that. By five o'clock she had changed her mind a dozen times about his invitation. At that point she was prepared not to go. Little did she know that she was no match for a shiny black limousine and a liveried chauffeur, who tipped his hat as he saw her step through the revolving doors of the news building.

Quickly ensconced in the plush velvet interior of the vehicle, she leaned back to enjoy the unaccustomed luxury and the thrill of not knowing what awaited her. She was pleasantly surprised. The car drew up to an elegant restaurant, the Villa d'Este, where the restaurant's doorman beat the mayor's chauffeur to the rear door of the car. Bobbie was not used to having attendance danced upon her and she thought she rather enjoyed it. The maître d' ushered her with a deferential bow to a corner table, where the mayor was rising to greet her.

"Ah, so I meet my nemesis." He smiled.

"Am I supposed to curtsy?" Bobbie answered dourly, though she knew not why.

"Only if we're doing a square dance," he answered. "So, you're Bobbie Schaeffer."

"I don't look like Eleanor Roosevelt, do I?"

"That was witty," he said. "I wanted a dinner date and here I find myself with a sparring partner instead."

"Dinner dates are generally requested, not commanded," she shot back.

He looked at her in exasperation. "Perhaps this was a mistake."

"If you'll call me a cab, I'll be glad to help you rectify it."

He sucked in a breath slowly. "This evening is on the brink of disaster, but I'm hungry, I'm tired, and you're a pretty girl, so I'm going to try to save it. So hello, Bobbie and I'm glad you came . . . I think."

"Mayor," she said as she inclined her head.

"Please call me Dan."

"As in, 'Hello, Mayor Dan.' "

"No, as in 'Hey, Dan, you're a pretty nice guy.' "

"Are you?" she asked with a half smile.

"You could stick around and find out. Would you like something to drink?"

"A Bristol Cream would be fine."

He only had to raise an eyebrow and the waiter was at his side.

"A Bristol for the lady and I'll have a Jack Daniel's." He turned to her and grinned as the waiter bowed and made his way from the table.

"Bobbie Schaeffer," the mayor said sternly, "are you trying to ruin me?"

"I most certainly am," she answered. To her amazement, he roared with laughter.

"Nobody can ruin me. I'm clean as a whistle. But it's awfully wicked of you—and cute—to admit that you've taken on so monumental a task."

"It's not monumental," she snapped. "And I'm not cute!"

He leaned over to remove her glasses. "You're right. You're beautiful."

21

"Mayor, you cannot buy my silence with a compliment and a dinner."

"That wasn't my intention. But perhaps it should be. Then I would have an excuse to dine with you tomorrow night too."

"Let's just get through tonight, okay?" she said with an impish smile. "And by the way, can I have my glasses back?"

"Of course." He laughed. "I like your cartoons. They're funny. They are misleading, but definitely funny. You should be working on Madison Avenue."

She clicked her tongue. "Can't get rid of me that way either."

"Truce," he said, grinning and holding up his hands in front of him. "No more shop talk."

"Nice weather we're having," she said mockingly.

"We don't have to talk about the weather either. Hmm, tell me, are you a good conversationalist?"

"When I want to be."

"And how do you feel now?"

"I think," she said slowly, "that *you* ought to work at it. Things come too easily for you."

"I'm sorry you feel that way. It's not at all true. I'm a workaholic. That's probably why I have no real friends and I'm not married."

"Oh, the poor mayor!"

He shook his head. "There's no way to touch second base with you."

"That's because I don't play ball."

"Touché." He laughed. "I'm starved. May I order for you?" She nodded. Again he only had to look up and the waiter who hovered just out of earshot was at his elbow.

"We'll start with the oysters Rockefeller, then two lobsters, steamed, about two pounds. And a bottle of Dom

Pérignon '76 with that. Is that all right with you?" he asked Bobbie.

"It beats a Big Mac."

He looked into her eyes. Her heart was pounding. Her fingers smarted from the tight grip she had on the seat of her chair.

"Tell me about yourself," he insisted.

"I'm forty-five, the mother of twelve, and I've buried six husbands."

"Can't you be serious?" he asked gently.

She pursed her lips quizzically. "I'll try. I'm twenty-seven and this job is my first big break. I'm a slow starter."

"The best often comes last," he said. "Married?"

She shook her head. "Never was and never will be."

"Oh-ho. Then we have at least one thing in common. What's your reason?"

She was thoughtful. "Mr. Right never came along and now I've worked too hard to get where I am to want to give it up in order to starch someone else's shirts and salt—"

"And pepper his eggs," Dan said in unison with her.

They laughed. For the first time that evening Bobbie felt at ease. She was, despite herself, impressed that he could joke about a cartoon that would make most politicians furious.

"Maybe you're a good egg, after all," Bobbie conceded.

"I don't know about that, but at least I'm not a rotten egg." Dan smiled. "I wonder why I've never run into you before. Are you a Milwaukee girl?"

"Born and bred. I went East for a while, after Mom and Dad died, but something called me back here. Maybe it was roots, but I think it had to do with the honesty of this town. The only example of corruption in government that I remember was when the county commissioner used his franking privileges to send personal mail."

23

"Oh, yes, that guy was a fool." He paused as the waiter arrived with the oysters Rockefeller and unobtrusively served them, first to Bobbie, then Dan. "So you're on your own."

She nodded. "I can handle it. Anyway, I have a sister in Fond du Lac, a glamorous, chic, married sister. We're as different as day and night, but I could always count on her to bring me a home-cooked meal if I were laid up with the flu."

"You could be glamorous if you wanted."

"That's just it; I don't want to. And you don't have to try and make me believe that I am beautiful. I'm not and I don't care." Surprised that she was talking so openly, Bobbie felt herself blush.

"I think you could use a little softening around the edges and someone to take care of you."

"Are you applying for the job?"

"It sounds tempting, although I'll settle for an evening's pleasure right now. You see, I'm busy taking care of a million people. And doing it rather well, I might add."

"Are you supposed to be the judge of that?"

"My name, *Dan,* means 'the judge.' "

"And mine means 'turtle dove,' but I'm not about to fly away, although maybe I should."

"At least wait until after the lobster," he said.

"Judge, uh, I mean Mayor, that's the best thing you've said tonight."

"I told you to call me Dan; please do."

"These oysters are delicious, Dan."

"One of the perks of the job is the food."

"Does the city pick up the tab?"

"Usually, and when they don't, they provide the best chefs for in-home dining. Tonight is on me though, not the city. This isn't strictly a business dinner."

"Too much rich food isn't good for you," Bobbie said

primly. *Although it doesn't look like it's hurting you one bit,* she thought. She had trouble ungluing her eyes from her companion. She thought she had never before seen, let alone dined with, so dashing a man. The way his eyes danced when he spoke, the way his curly black hair fell boyishly over them, the way he hunched his wide shoulders, would put Robert Redford to shame, and it gave him a positively unfair advantage over anyone he was with. He had told her that she was beautiful. Hah! Next to him she felt drab and even homely.

"What do you mean by not *strictly* a business dinner?" Bobbie asked as the realization of what he had said hit her. Two waiters came over at that moment, one with lobster bibs and the other with two platters of the biggest lobsters Bobbie had ever seen.

"These must be three pounders at least," she said, hungrily eyeing the red shellfish on her plate as one waiter loosely tied the bib around her neck. The other waiter smilingly asked if he could crack the claws for them.

"Leave the nutcrackers here," Dan said. "I'll take care of myself and the lady." After one waiter finished pouring the champagne, the mayor waved them away.

With her first bite of the sweet white lobster, Bobbie closed her eyes in exaggerated ecstasy. "Mmmm, this is my favorite food in the world!"

"Well, I propose a toast before the feast."

"Oh, gosh, I should have waited," Bobbie apologized. She felt herself blush at her faux pas.

"Not at all. Your enthusiasm is refreshing."

Bobbie thought she heard a patronizing ring to his voice. But when he held up his glass, she lifted hers.

"To lovely Bobbie, to honor in the media, and to His Honor—me."

"Well, that's original," Bobbie said dryly. "To pick up where we left off. You said this was not strictly a business

25

dinner. We've covered the amenities, so why don't you get on with business?"

"I could have let public relations handle this but I wanted to have the pleasure. It's not often that I encounter so alluring an opponent. I'm going to explain the economics of your day-care center to you and the psychology of a people who need their government to hold their hand every step of the way—"

"I don't need you to teach me anything!" Bobbie exploded. The butter-dipped lobster turned rancid in her mouth. She was heartsick, for she felt that she had allowed herself to be conned. How absurd it had been to entertain the thought for even a moment that he could be interested in her when he could have every gorgeous, brilliant female from here to Tuscaloo at his fingertips if he so desired. All he wanted was to manipulate the media!

"And I don't think I'm hungry anymore." She got hastily to her feet. "I'll take a cab!"

"You certainly do need me to teach you something— manners!"

"Manners are one thing, hypocrisy is another!" she said over her shoulder as she flounced out of the restaurant.

The cool night air slapped against her moist brow, making her shiver uncontrollably as she stood under the red awning at the restaurant's entrance. The doorman, having just ushered in an elderly couple, turned to her with a sycophantic smile. When he heard her request for a taxi, his smile faded, for he remembered who her dinner companion had been and nobody but nobody left the mayor flat. His shrill whistle brought a yellow and white vehicle posthaste, and his smile was restored when he glanced down at the generous tip that Bobbie placed in his palm.

Bobbie thought it odd how the limelight, even its reflected glare, made your private life public property.

The old patched seats of the cab, the reeking odor of

ancient cigars that clung to the interior, and the fat, grizzled face of the cabbie were a far cry from the chariot that had brought her here, but to Bobbie, at that moment, it was a haven, for in it she wore no blinders. She saw who was in front of her and she knew who she was.

Her emotions were a mixture of anger, hurt (though she refused to admit that to herself), and embarrassment. How dare he pretend to like her, shower her with compliments, and wine and dine her as a ruse to brainwash her to his point of view. And what a dolt she was to have been led on like that, even if only for a short time. Well, she'd better get used to it; she wasn't the marrying kind. It was her sister's type that men liked: pretty, sugary girls who looked up at them with adoring eyes. Bobbie was cut out for a career. Maybe she'd wind up rich or famous. She had the talent. And at any rate no man was going to make a fool of her again. She had gone through that in her early twenties and then again tonight. At least she had recognized it early and escaped. Mayor Dan Allen would soon learn that she would not fall for that line of his about taking off her glasses and discovering a beauty. For, if she had anything to do with it, her cartoons would help end his upcoming campaign for reelection with a whimper, and she would certainly get a bang out of that!

CHAPTER III

Bobbie awoke the next morning feeling groggy and unrefreshed. An unusually sound sleeper, she could not understand her insomnia of the last two nights. Something was bothering her, and it nagged at her mind through breakfast and on the way to work, but once she arrived at the news building, whatever the problem, it was replaced by a fresh annoyance. Hermani was standing in the center of the floor, surrounded by a city reporter, an ad man, and a secretary. They, with the exception of Hermani, looked up guiltily as Bobbie entered.

"Ah, here she is, the mayor's new consort," Hermani dripped silkily. "So how vas he, dahling? Is he as good as they say?"

Bobbie glared in answer. She reached her desk with a churning stomach and the beginnings of a headache. She opened the morning press releases that were piled in front of her and started reading. But she was not to be spared. Larry, a young beat reporter, sashayed over to her and giggled.

"I just heard the news. Oh, I'm so excited for you. The mayor's new sweetheart! Tell me about it. How did you ever wangle an invitation from him in the first place?"

"Calm down," Bobbie replied sharply. "I am nobody's sweetheart. Someone has been spreading malicious gossip,

28

and I've an idea who it is," she added, almost as an after-thought.

"What do you mean? You were out with him last night. It's in the newspaper. I read it. There's a picture too," he said ingenuously.

"What!" Bobbie exploded. "Not our paper?"

"No, it's in the *Gazette*. Hold on, I'll get you a copy." He ran to a shelf and held out the morning edition of the competition.

Bobbie sank down in her chair as she stared at the picture of her and the mayor downing a fluted glass of champagne. *I look like a sick cow,* she thought despairingly. The caption was even worse: "Mayor makes inroads with press. Is the new love in his life the up-and-coming cartoonist of Milwaukee's leading afternoon daily? If she's not, the sparkle in their eyes could have fooled us!"

"Well," Larry exclaimed, "the secret is out. And you're one lucky lady. Ask him if he has a younger brother, will you?"

Bobbie laughed in spite of herself and shook her head. "This is all a mistake. It was a business dinner."

"All right, I can understand," Larry said, grinning slyly. "There are some secrets that are simply too delicious to share."

Bobbie flashed a broad smile at him. He was irrepressible, but it was impossible to be angry with him.

"Go back to work, kid. There's nothing to tell, but I promise you this: If there ever is, you'll be the first to know."

"That's a deal," Larry agreed and he left to roam about the office, doing more listening in on conversations than polishing his trade. There was no time for Bobbie to ponder this unlikely turn of events, for no sooner had Larry left than he was back telling her that the chief wanted to see her.

"Good morning, Bobbie," Nesbitt greeted her cordially. "Can I get you a cup of coffee?"

"No, thank you," Bobbie said, shaking her head. She was puzzled. This wasn't the editor-in-chief's style. She could feel anxiety creeping in on her as she frantically thought of the reason for this talk. Much to Bobbie's relief, the chief came straight to the point.

"I hear you were out with Allen last night. Good work. I don't know how you managed it, that's your business. But I presume you're going to be working here a long time and that you have your priorities straight. We haven't had the inside track on City Hall since he got himself elected. If you can ferret out some information, like just how he plans on giving the police force more muscle, this paper would be mighty grateful to you. I don't have to tell you that we are the major liberal force in Milwaukee and our business is two-fold. One, we give 'em the news straight, and two, we get the goods on the riffraff presently occupying City Hall and we get them out! Allen has four more months to campaign before he's up for reelection. That doesn't give us a hell of a lot of time, so we're out there, no holds barred. I'm counting on you, Bobbie. You're part of the team." Bobbie felt her stomach catapult as the import of his words struck her.

"Are you asking me to spy on him, sir?"

"Don't play with words. We've got a job to do here. You're on this team or you're not," Nesbitt answered impatiently.

He wasn't going to make it easier for Bobbie, that was sure. He wanted her for a stool pigeon and if she wanted a job, a stool pigeon she would be.

"Understand?" he asked curtly as Bobbie remained standing mutely.

"I think so," Bobbie said, nodding. She backed away till

she felt the doorknob jab her in the small of her back. Nesbitt had just lit up a pipe, and the aroma of sweet cherry tobacco that assailed her nostrils as she turned and hurried to her cubicle seemed at odds with the unscrupulous face he had just shown her. A small fire of rebellion lit up Bobbie's insides and troubled her. The cause was a good one. She, too, preferred to see a liberal city administration restored to power and, goodness knows, she owed the mayor nothing, except perhaps the market price for a lobster dinner and a swift kick. Then why, she wondered, did she feel reluctant, angry even, at Nesbitt's proposal? It was simple, she concluded after a soul-searching half hour. She didn't like being ordered around, she hated authority, and Nesbitt was coming on like a classic Boss Man. It had nothing at all to do with the mayor. That decided, she breathed a sigh of relief, which quickly turned to one of despair as she realized that she still didn't know what she was going to do. The bottom line was her job. If she wanted to keep it, she knew what she had to do, and if she didn't, there were hundreds of eager applicants panting for the chance to wear her shoes. But, she laughed mockingly to herself, she wasn't that sort of girl. Anyway, she was a terrible liar. Knowing herself, she'd probably develop a rash and walk up to the mayor wearing a big embroidered S on her dress—for Stoolie. She picked up a pencil and looked at the blank sheet of paper on her desk. She would decide later. Right now there was a cartoon to get done.

Time sped by as Bobbie sketched. During that time nothing existed for her except paper, ink, and her imagination. As usual there grew around her a small mountain of crumpled-up papers, for, where her work was concerned, Bobbie was a perfectionist. Her personal papers were never where they were supposed to be, but her work was always orderly and precise. A line that she considered a fraction too wide, and she would unhesitatingly discard an afternoon's work. She bit her bottom lip in concentration.

Spring was in the air and Bobbie allowed herself to wax poetic as she depicted the seasonal change from the bitter, gray ogre, Winter, to the mild-mannered piper, Spring. In a decidedly nonpolitical frame of mind Bobbie welcomed the uncontroversial topic and she was sure her readers would appreciate her versatility. She had discovered that the newspaper was receiving calls about her and that she already had a small following. The simplicity of her technique, the boldness of her line, and the power of her message was fast making hers one of the most noticed spots in the paper.

Gratified and proud though she was, Bobbie still had to survive in the petty world of office politics. Even as she straightened her desk after a hard day's work, she quaked at the thought that Hermani might be out there waiting to corner her as she made for the exit. It was worse. Hermani alone was a trial, but Hermani holding court was insufferable. In an encore of the morning performance Hermani called out well within earshot of Nesbitt, Larry, and everyone else who worked on the *Milwaukee Post*, "Careful tonight, honey. Your friend is a heartbreaker and a hunter. We want the trophy on our wall, not his. Isn't that right, Cal?" Nesbitt either did not hear it or chose to ignore the bait.

Feeling the blood pulse through her head and feeling uncomfortably warm, Bobbie wished for the thousandth time that she had the sangfroid to chasten the Hermanis of this world. Instead, and much to her later embarrassment, she fairly skulked out of the office, thinking that if she had a tail it would be between her legs like a cornered animal. Out in the hallway of the monolithic structure that housed the offices of the paper, she leaned heavily on

32

the elevator button with a clenched fist. She heard foot-steps behind her and turned to meet Larry's look of consternation.

"Don't let her get to you, Bobbie. Everyone knows she's a jerk."

"People listen to jerks too," Bobbie replied.

"Nonsense! No one takes her seriously, and after you walked out, Nesbitt called her into his office. And he looked pretty grim."

Bobbie grinned suddenly and squeezed Larry's arm.

"Thanks. I feel better already. See you tomorrow," she said as she stepped into the open elevator.

Her step was jaunty as she walked out to her car. It was interesting, she thought as she belted her London Fog against the blustery March wind, how a kind word could restore one's good humor. In fact she felt so good, inexplicably, she mused, when she remembered the dilemma facing her, that she decided to try the little gourmet take-out store that had intrigued her each time she walked to the parking lot at night. The chicken curry looked tempting, the imported chutney exotic, and how nice it would be not to cook tonight. The man behind the counter, a roly-poly French expatriate, smiled and flirted with her as he deftly packaged her order and made change for the twenty she handed him.

"*Bon appétit!*" he called as she picked up the brown bag.

"*Merci* and *bonne nuit*," she responded in her school-book French. "I knew there was reason to take French for four years," she muttered to herself while hurrying once more through the windswept street.

She was glad to get home. Her apartment was cheery, the food was superbly spiced, the music—a Neil Diamond album she put on the stereo—was soothing, and yet some-how, walking through the kitchen to the living room,

33

touching the leaves of her jade plant, and flipping through the pages of her latest subscription magazine, she felt rather lonely. It was a feeling she was unaccustomed to, and one she didn't like.

CHAPTER IV

Bobbie was gratified to note that Hermani wore a chastened look the next day. Larry was probably right about Nesbitt calling her down on her behavior toward Bobbie. That she had harbored reservations about coming into work this morning seemed absurd now, for no one paid her untoward attention. She was not, she reminded herself, the center of the universe, and for that she was very glad. People cared about their own problems, whether their coffee was too cold or too sweet, and not about her alleged affair with Mr. Marvelous Mayor.

Her nose was buried in the morning paper when Jerry Greene, a staff photographer, stuck his head through her door.

"You doing anything tonight?"

"Not that I know of," she answered. She liked Jerry. He was a comfortable, full-bearded man with a slight paunch to tell his tale of Sunday television sports and beer.

"Cal"—Jerry was on a first-name basis with everyone—"gave me an extra ticket to the Pabst Theatre Fund Raising Ball tonight. You've got first dibs for being new here and sweet. Larry is coming too. I like being surrounded by ingenues."

"You mean sophisticates," Bobbie joked. "It sounds great. Maybe I'll get some ammunition for a cartoon."

"Now you're talking like a real newspaperwoman. Never pass up any opportunities."

"Thanks, Jerry."

"We'll meet here at eight thirty and go in my car. And, by the way, it's formal dress."

"Formal dress!" Bobbie stood openmouthed.

"Don't worry." Jerry grinned. "You'd look great in a formal potato sack."

"I wish I had the same confidence in myself," she scowled good-naturedly. "In any case I'll be here, and thanks again. I mean it."

"Not to worry." He hustled out with his Nikon swinging from his shoulder.

Settling back in her chair, Bobbie tried to apply herself to her work, but all she could think of was what to wear that evening. Not wanting to waste her time on trivia, she told herself that it didn't matter what she wore, for she wasn't going to be a principal at the ball; she was only the press. *But even the press can't look like a total frump,* she argued with herself. Sighing, she mentally sifted through her wardrobe. The only two things that could be called formals were inappropriate. One, a relic from her senior prom, was a frothy, frilly pink thing. The other, a bridesmaid dress that she wore at her sister's wedding, was in kelly green with scalloped sleeves and a demure neckline and looked like it belonged in church, which it did. Perhaps she could wear her black velvet suit.

Justifying to herself her three-o'clock departure from the newsroom with her limp hair, she hastened home to prepare for the evening. As a representative of the *Milwaukee Post,* she should have gleaming, silky tresses, even if her apparel would leave something to be desired.

Stepping out of the shower in her steamy bathroom, Bobbie shivered in anticipation of the evening. She was a devotee of the theater and admired those in the profession,

36

and the Pabst Theatre, a truly imposing structure, gave Milwaukee a veneer of culture. No longer was it necessary to make the two-hour trip to Chicago to see fine theater. The Pabst attracted the best artists from all over the country.

Bobbie looked at herself in the mirror with satisfaction. Her skin was rosy from toweling but still dewy from the steam. Slim waisted, with firm, pert breasts and long, slender legs, her body, she noted, wasn't half bad. With one hand she swept her hair to the top of her head and with the other she pulled long tendrils down over her ears. She looked, even to herself, quite engaging.

"It's not Brigitte Bardot," she murmured to her reflection, "but it's not Phyllis Diller either." She decided to be daring and to wear her hair knotted, and she even broke down and wore the contact lenses that lay unused in the medicine cabinet. As she mascaraed her lashes she puzzled over her actions. She didn't care how she looked. She never had, and she certainly didn't want to impress Jerry or Larry. And heaven knows, she wasn't expecting to be the belle of the ball. Anyway, looks didn't matter. She was gifted; she had drive, ambition. Those were the important things. Even so, she was pleased at the transformation she had wrought. She had gone into the shower bespectacled and—well, healthy looking. She emerged rather dazzling. Now if she only had something decent to wear. . . . She got out her black velvet suit and studied it doubtfully when inspiration struck. Years ago her mother had brought her a floor-length sarong from Hawaii. Though it was a striking frock, in stark white with only a single bold purple stripe running diagonally from the one covered shoulder to the hem, Bobbie had folded it and put it in her drawer and forgotten about it. It wasn't her style, something her mother had known but had always tried to change. Now Bobbie lifted it out of the tissue paper pro-

37

tecting it from the tangled garments heaped on top. She knelt at her closet to find her high-heeled gold sandals her mother had given her to complete the ensemble. As she looked at herself with her new hairdo, new face, and this dress, which clung sensuously to the curves of her hips and bosom, she thought for the first time that maybe her mother and the mayor were right. She possessed the raw material of beauty. And natural resources were only given in order to be developed. The trench coat that she wore over her shoulders would not have appeared in *Vogue,* but Bobbie was certain that she had no cashmere wraps secreted away at the bottom of another drawer.

Bobbie arrived at the office at 8:30 P.M. on the dot and was greeted by a long low wolf whistle as Jerry eyed her with obvious approval.

"I think I know your sister. She works here as a cartoonist."

"You're a real card," Bobbie laughed. "Do I look that different?"

"Does the 'Mona Lisa' look different from Van Gogh's self-portrait?"

"Well, that's a backhanded compliment if I ever heard one," Bobbie retorted in a miffed tone.

"I didn't mean it the way it sounds. You always look nice, but tonight you're a knockout."

Bobbie smiled. "Here comes Larry."

"Hi, gang," Larry greeted them. "You look gorgeous, Bobbie."

"Thanks. So do you," she returned, admiring his light gray tux.

"My chariot awaits," Jerry said, ushering them into one of the few banged-up red VW Bugs with a sunroof still to be seen in the streets of Milwaukee.

The ride to the theater was short and bumpy. Mercedeses, Rolls-Royces, and Cadillacs lined the curb in

38

front. Bobbie felt a surge of exhilaration as she walked up the light-bathed steps of the theater with her friends. Attendance at functions such as this was a decided plus to her job. Just as they entered, an attendant came to check their coats for them. Bobbie gladly gave hers up. The opulence with which the lobby was decorated was stunning. Flowers of every description decked the walls, framed the windows, and were given as boutonnieres or nosegays to each guest and even to the press.

With their press passes out, Jerry, Larry, and Bobbie were acknowledged as legitimate guests, shown to one of the two tables set up in the back of the room, and left peremptorily to fend for themselves.

"There's a conspicuous dearth of flowers on this table," Jerry commented wryly.

"The ashtray in the center will do just as well," Bobbie responded tongue in cheek.

"And there's nothing to get in the way of your camera lens," Larry joined in.

"Kind of them to be so considerate," Bobbie added.

"Can I get you two a drink?" Jerry offered gallantly.

"I think I'd rather get my own," Bobbie said. "That way maybe I can get an angle on an overheard conversation."

"Where are your scruples?" Jerry asked in mock horror.

"The same place as every other newsperson's."

"I don't know how you do it, Bobbie. All a journalist has to do is write a coherent, factual story; you have to turn it into something funny and clever with maybe a one-liner to get the point across."

"You know what they say"—Bobbie smiled modestly— "'A picture is worth a thousand words.'"

Jerry moved to the side. He checked his equipment and

39

nodded. "What do you say we rejoin ranks again when they serve dinner?"

"Sounds good." Bobbie nodded. "Later." She winked at Larry. Picking up a glass of white wine from a passing waiter, Bobbie surveyed the throng at the hors d'oeuvres buffet. It was funny how voracious even the very rich became when the food was unlimited. Unaware of the many lecherous stares she was attracting from intoxicated husbands and the scowls she was receiving from their wives, Bobbie moseyed here and there on the crowded floor. The snatches of conversation about golf pros, stock options, and caterers that reached her ears were singularly uninteresting. That and the backslapping between the men and the one-liners that some of them threw at the female companions of others soon melted together into one incomprehensible din.

She was startled then when she felt, rather than heard, the hush fall over the crowd. Turning in the direction of their stares, she almost fell as she saw Mayor Dan Allen, his bronzed face (a feat in itself in frigid Wisconsin) wreathed in smiles, stride through the gilded doors to the center of the room, where his table was slightly raised on a low platform. The power he exuded was so great that Bobbie caught her breath and felt paralyzed for an instant, though all she wanted to do was run for the nearest exit. She noticed from the corner of her eye the deferential expressions on the faces of even the most pompous-appearing guests and felt strangely proud. Why she should feel anything remotely connected to pride was a puzzle to her and made her doubt her sanity.

After a moment's thought she realized that she could not skulk out the back, for Jerry and Larry would either be worried sick or, worse, guess the reason. If only she had a pill that would make her invisible. Moving quickly, she arrived at the empty press table where she shrank down

40

in her seat and prayed she would go unnoticed. With the mayor's arrival dinner was ceremoniously served. In a daze she barely heard the chitchat around her or tasted the medallions of beef on her plate.

Larry nudged her. "What's the matter? You look like you've seen a ghost. Uh," he remarked after a pause, "I guess you have. You haven't spoken to him yet, have you?" Bobbie shook her head.

"Does he know you're here?" Larry pursued his line of questioning.

"No, and I don't think I'm going to give him the chance to find out." She leaned over to Jerry. "Do you mind if I leave, and could you walk me out to the bus stop?" She smiled winsomely.

"You're forever running out on me," a deep voice resonated behind her ear.

Whirling around in her seat, Bobbie paled. "Hello, Dan."

"Are you collecting material for another caricature, or are you following me?"

"Your first guess is on target," she replied frostily.

"I would have preferred the second," he flirted. Recovering her poise, she introduced an attentive Jerry and Larry to the mayor.

"Any friend of Bobbie's . . ." he joked with them.

"Can I quote you on that, Mayor?" Jerry asked.

"It's strictly off the record," he jested back. He held out a hand to Bobbie as the first strains of the band music floated out across the floor.

"Care to dance?"

Though she ignored the proffered hand, Bobbie stood up and walked silently onto the dance floor. Her heart was thumping painfully. As he took her in his arms his eyes flickered quickly over her. They moved from her eyes to her neck, over her shoulders, and lingered for a split sec-

41

ond over the rise of her breasts. Bobbie wished fervently that she had gone along with her first impulse and worn her black velvet suit, for under his eyes, in her flimsy cotton sarong, she felt naked and exposed, and it was not lost upon her that two hundred other eyes were avidly watching Dan Allen mentally undress her.

"I was right," he whispered in her ear. "You are stunning."

Bobbie acknowledged the compliment with a tight smile, which he couldn't see, for he whirled across the floor in perfectly executed style. His powerful muscles pulsed shamelessly against the palm that lay lightly on his shoulder. As she felt his hard thighs move against her to the soft cadences of a Barbara Streisand piece, she realized with a jolt that this man could too easily sweep her away to lands hitherto unknown.

The band moved from one number to the next without stopping, and Dan Allen never slackened his grip on her. He was a born dancer and a born leader. And so it was with a sinking heart that the terrifying thought that she was born to follow him struck Bobbie. Never before had she glided so easily to music. She rarely danced. But the signals he gave her, the slight pressures he exerted on her arm or waist, were so universally comprehensible that they almost seemed color coded. They flowed together as in a dream.

"Mmmm, my pretty," he whispered in her ear, "you're stepping on my toe."

Bobbie jumped back. "Oh, no! I'm sorry. Did I hurt you?" Dan looked wryly down at his feet. He lifted his left foot off the floor and wriggled it.

"Nothing broken. Give me a smile and I'll be as good as new."

"Why don't we sit this one out. I'm tired anyway."

42

"I'm just getting warmed up," he protested. "And I think you are too," he added insinuatingly.

"Listen, I'm sorry I stepped on your toe but that doesn't mean we have to draw out this painful encounter," she snapped.

"Was that intentional?" he asked laughingly. "Or are you one of these witty people who make unconscious puns?"

"I'll let you know after I sign up for a psychology course," she replied acidly.

"Come now, the pain you're inflicting on my ego is worse than the pain in my foot."

"I doubt if anything could pierce your ego."

"What do you have against me?" Dan looked at her, bewildered.

"Let's just say that I don't enjoy being used," Bobbie answered quickly.

"Is that what you think?" Dan threw back his head and laughed so loud that it caused several heads to turn once more in their direction.

"My dear, I have bigger fish to fry, and I told you I like your caricatures. They keep me in the public eye and there's nothing dearer to a politician's heart."

"Well then, what was the reason for the dinner?" she asked, slightly mollified.

"Need you ask? I'm a man and you're a delightful woman. I like your honesty. It's refreshing." With one hand he traced a line from her eyebrows to the tip of her chin. Involuntarily she shivered. "Let's leave," he said suddenly.

"You can't!" she gasped. "You're the guest of honor. Don't you have to make a speech?"

"I just had to make an appearance here. And I have done that. I've even made a spectacle. I'm not in the mood for another one of these functions tonight," he added sardonically. "And you're my ticket out of here. You know how it goes, Playboy Mayor and Pretty Girl."

He led her back to her table and drew up a chair. Just as he was opening his mouth to make apologies to Jerry and Larry, a youngish, though balding, little man in wire-rimmed glasses and Ivy League tweeds ran up to him and whispered urgently in his ear.

"Relax, Coleman," Dan said expansively. He turned to Bobbie. "Coleman here is my top aide and he's ready to blow a gasket because of my—harrumph—conduct on the dance floor."

"I can't say that I blame him," Bobbie said dryly.

"Elliot Coleman, say hello to the people," Dan commanded lightly. "This is Bobbie Schaeffer, Jerry Greene, and Larry Gynt."

Elliot sniffed and glared. "Mayor, they're waiting for you on the dais."

"Tell them to go on without me. They said no speeches, and I feel even less like listening to one than giving one. Give me your car keys, Coleman. You go on home in the limo."

Elliot Coleman's Adam's apple bobbed up and down, reminding Bobbie of a turkey ready for the slaughter. "I would consider that injudicious as well as indiscreet, Mayor."

"I don't give a damn what you consider it. I have something more important on my mind." He shot a sidelong glance at Bobbie.

"Will you be saying the same thing when the Fine Arts Caucus endorses the other candidate in the next election?" Coleman asked between pursed lips.

"The keys, please." Dan rolled his eyes upward. Reluctantly reaching in his back pocket, Coleman handed over his car keys.

"Don't forget, tomorrow morning, eight sharp, you

44

have a meeting with the head of Local Six-one-nine. Try to get him behind you on the police issue and tell him we'll go for his city contract." Spinning on his heel, Coleman left to speak to the director of the Theatre Guild without so much as a nod in Bobbie's direction.

"A charming fellow," Bobbie commented.

"Don't pay attention to Coleman. He's all work and no play."

"Perhaps he's right. You may ruffle some feathers if you leave this early."

"And they'll be smooth again as soon as they get what they want," Dan said, shrugging his broad shoulders. "Anyway, enough people had their picture taken with me to assuage any sensibilities."

"If I didn't know better, I would say you're a cynic," Bobbie smiled.

"I'm glad you know better. Come on, I need some fresh air."

Bobbie and Dan Allen took their leave of Jerry and Larry, who sat openmouthed, hanging on to every word that was exchanged between the mayor and their co-worker. Dan ushered Bobbie out to the cloakroom, where he retrieved her raincoat and laid it around her shoulders.

"Thanks for helping me get out of there. I'm usually better at these functions," he admitted apologetically, "but the contrast between so many hollow words and"— he fumbled for the word—"your unpretentiousness struck me hard. I like that you don't want anything from me except maybe to take me down a peg."

Bobbie's pulse quickened as she remembered Cal Nesbitt's orders to worm her way into Dan's life in order to collect damaging information. As he took her arm gently in his hand, she swallowed hard and fell in step beside him.

Luckily Elliot Coleman's car was parked right in front

of the theater in an illegal space. That was one car that wouldn't get a ticket, Bobbie thought. Long ago she had read that cars reflected their owners' personalities, and sitting in Coleman's drab green no-nonsense sedan, she could well believe it. Her thoughts were interrupted when the car started with a lurch. Dan followed the lake to the center of town and Bobbie sat peacefully, enjoying the nighttime view.

"Do you mind if we just drive around for a while before I take you home?" he asked.

"Not at all. I like driving at night, if I'm in the passenger seat."

In the pale light of the moon the large lake mansions loomed with a haunting beauty. He drove leisurely, all the while commenting proudly on the wide, handsome streets. He stopped at the pier and nosed the car to the very edge so they saw, over the hood, the black water lapping up over the gray wood of the rickety-looking structure. In the distance the lighthouse beckoned with its twinkling flashes.

"There's something magical about water at night, about the sound of it lapping against the shore," Bobbie said in a low voice.

"I'm a great one for views. I have a cabin on a lake up north. If only I could get up there more often . . ." he said wistfully.

"Why don't you?"

"I have responsibilities," Dan replied loftily.

"Oh, pardon me," Bobbie snapped in a sarcastic voice.

"You know, you're too sensitive and you have a quick temper," Dan remarked.

"You have a quicker tongue," she shot back.

"I don't want to argue with you now—"

"We'll save that for later," Bobbie broke in with a half smile.

46

"The Pieces of Eight is just up the strip." Dan gestured toward the well-known waterfront restaurant. "Would you like a drink?"

Bobbie shook her head. "I've had enough velvet, gold, and crystal for one night. If you want, I can fix you something up at my place."

"I like the way that sounds," Dan said, arching his brows and grinning mischievously.

Bobbie blushed. "You have the wrong impression. I'm inviting you for a drink and that's all," she said emphatically.

"In my book that was the right impression, but you're the boss," Dan chuckled. Bobbie felt a stab of annoyance. He wasn't taking her seriously.

"Anyway," he continued, "that's perfectly all right with me. I'm starved for some intelligent female companionship and *you* look good enough to eat!"

"Must you make these sexual innuendos all the time?"

"What other kind are there?"

"Is this conduct befitting the mayor of our great city?" she asked tongue in cheek.

He beat his chest à la King Kong. "The protector of the city gates, the savior of Wisconsin, and"—he laughed— "the vanquisher of beautiful young women."

"You are wrong on three counts: I'm not so young, I'm not beautiful, and I'm not about to be vanquished by anyone, let alone you!"

"You're a woman with spunk. I like that."

"Is there anything you don't like about women? With the trail of broken hearts you've left behind you, one would think you were rather indiscriminate in your tastes."

"My reputation has a life of its own. It has little to do with reality."

Bobbie raised her eyebrows. "To change the subject,

47

how are you going to deal with the threatened policemen's strike?"

"Are you playing at Mata Hari?" Dan teased. "Trying to force my political secrets out in the open?"

Awash in a mix of emotions, Bobbie was unable to answer. He didn't know how near to the truth he was and how relieved she was that he wasn't going to give her the opportunity to fulfill Cal Nesbitt's expectations. In an effort to relieve the tension she felt, she quickly changed the subject.

"I smell spring in the air," Bobbie said in a voice that sounded to her own ears strained and unnatural.

"The thaw is finally upon us." Dan breathed deeply of the misty night air. Suddenly he asked, "Do you like cannolis? I know a great little Italian bakery near here."

"Sure. We did miss dessert, didn't we?"

"We did. But you look good enough to eat."

"Dan!"

"Sorry about that again. I get carried away sometimes," he confessed with a fetching grin.

Bobbie gripped the seat, for she never would have backed a car up so quickly on the narrow slatted pier. The vehicle screeched in protest as he turned it onto the street. He drove with an easy expertise that marked whatever he did, she thought.

Milwaukee, seen through Dan Allen's eyes, took on a new color. It seemed exciting and fresh, unspoiled yet cosmopolitan. He took a long circuitous route to her house, passing on the way the museum and Wildcat Stadium. It was with great pride that he expounded on the attractions of the city. Though Bobbie was familiar with almost everything he said about it, she let him ramble on, for he was clearly enjoying it and she liked to listen to him speak. He used picturesque expressions that would have

48

seemed more appropriate falling off the lips of a librarian. She asked him when he was planning a vacation.

"When I dot my *i*'s and cross my *t*'s and get my life in order." She liked that.

"I understand you're a piano player," she said.

"You've been doing your homework. Piano relaxes me. If I had the talent, I'd be playing in Carnegie Hall now."

"Maybe you will—in another life," she bantered.

He pulled over suddenly in a narrow alleyway. He banged on a locked iron door.

"This is the back door to the bakery," he explained. He checked his watch. "They should be there now baking tomorrow's batch."

"Mama Sirianni," he shouted. "Open up, it's Mayor Allen." The door opened a crack and a small round lady with gray wisps of hair peeping out from under an out-sized chef's hat looked out suspiciously. Her puckered mouth broke out in a smile as she spied Dan's face in the murky alley. Throwing open the door, she held her arms out and beamed.

"His Honor, the Mayor. Bennzo, come quick, look who's here. Come in, come in," she beckoned to Bobbie.

"Sit down, Your Honor. It's been a long time. You been dieting or what?"

"No, no, a diet couldn't keep me away from your ovens. It's work. I've been busy."

A rotund man, his face wreathed in smiles, came around the corner of an enormous black oven, still wiping his hands on his spotted white apron.

"Is that how you welcome His Honor, Maria?" he reproached his wife. "How do you do," He bowed to Bobbie. "Mayor, it's good to see you."

"Thanks, Bennzo. I told Miss Schaeffer about your cannolis. Are they still as good as I remember?"

"For you, they'll be better." He rushed off to a small

oven and lifted out a dozen of the pastries, then filled some with cheese and some with chocolate.

"Freeze what you can't finish," he said, pressing the package on the mayor. Dan fished his wallet out of his pocket.

"No, no, it's on the house. Our pleasure."

Dan left a ten-dollar bill on the counter. "I can't take it, Bennzo. You know that."

"You insult me." Bennzo looked crestfallen.

"The little lady is from the newspaper," he said in a whispered aside. Bobbie almost exploded with laughter.

"I can just see the headlines now," she said mirthfully after they were once more esconced in the car. " 'Probe Bribery at City Hall. Mayor Accused of Accepting Twelve Cannolis.' "

"That's how it starts," Dan responded in a serious tone. He passed the last few minutes of the short trip in silence.

"Nice town house," he finally said as he parked in front of Bobbie's apartment.

She didn't acknowledge the comment, for she was busy regretting her invitation. This was bound to be awkward. She would have regretted it even more had she seen the figure across the street move stealthily from behind a tree and snap three pictures in quick succession: of him helping her out of the car, walking to her door, and entering.

"Do you like living alone?" Dan asked as he surveyed her apartment.

"Very much. Do you?"

He nodded. "There's something to say for not being nagged and not having to answer to anyone. Although I might be persuaded to change that point of view."

"Not me," Bobbie replied archly. "I'm a confirmed bachelorette."

"Them's fightin' words, lady," Dan joked. "Now how about that drink you promised me?"

"Coming up, sir. I hope sherry is okay."

"Fine." He followed her into the narrow kitchenette, watched with a sardonic grin as she took the bottle of cream sherry out of the cupboard, rinsed the glasses, and clinked ice cubes into them. As she poured the amber liquid she became aware of his eyes traveling over her face, piercing the depths of her eyes, and stopping at the cupid's bow that formed her lips. She stood there, hypnotized, with the drinks in her hands. He walked slowly toward her then and his hands brushed her creamy white shoulders. She trembled as he traced the line of her spine, encircled her finally in two arms of enormous strength. Fear of her own desire to submit herself to this man overwhelmed her and she jerked away. As she did so the glass in her left hand slipped, as of its own volition, out of her grasp and down the front of the mayor's shirt, spilling sherry and ice.

"Aieee!" he exclaimed, springing back. "I guess I was wrong to think the spring thaw had arrived. It feels like the frost is still upon us!"

Bobbie reached for the roll of paper towels. She could feel the color suffuse her cheeks.

"I don't believe I did that," she apologized. "I'm not usually so clumsy." She held the paper towels out to him as he unbuttoned his shirt. Bobbie swallowed hard as she glimpsed the wide nut-brown expanse of chest covered with a veritable forest of curly black hairs. As he dried himself off he felt her intense gaze upon him; he sensed her longing.

"Come here, sweet lady," he whispered huskily. He pulled her against him and bent his head to kiss the soft white flesh at the base of her throat, and then his mouth fastened upon hers once more and with his teeth and his tongue he kissed her deeply.

She gasped as unfamiliar sensations started in her stomach and spread like fire throughout her body. How she

51

wanted to respond to him! Yet darkness, in the form of terror, overcame her. Even as a young girl she had sworn that she would be beholden to no one. She knew she didn't possess the feminine wiles to catch a man and so she refused to compete in a situation where she wasn't even in the running. She would not be vulnerable; she would not be the fool. And what really could Dan Allen want with her when he could have almost any woman in the country with the snap of his fingers? She sensed that Dan was a danger to her, for he embodied everything that she found admirable in a man: a deepness of soul, a keenness of mind, and overwhelming sexuality. Better to keep away from him. She would only be hurt in the end. With a muffled sob she tore herself away.

"Bobbie, what's the matter?"

"Nothing. Just leave me alone," she said, wide-eyed. She backed out of the kitchen and turned to run, though she was chagrined to note later that the farthest she could have run was the living room balcony. Hardly had she moved when his huge frame loomed over her. He pinned her arms to her sides.

"What's the matter?" he repeated.

Tears welled in her eyes. "I don't want a lover. I'm sorry."

"You could have fooled me," he said sardonically.

"You'd better leave," she whispered in a half sob.

"I will," he hissed, "after you give me an explanation."

Bobbie was no longer able to meet his eyes. Staring at the floor, she let hang between them a silence palpable with tension.

"I didn't think you were a game player," he said.

"Well, thanks for the evening," she said coolly.

He strode over to the door and let himself out without a backward glance. Bobbie stood rigidly, listening to the click of the door latch signal his exit from her life. She

52

stood like that for what seemed like an aeon, her mind a morass of contradicting thoughts. She felt angry, at him for what he must assume about her, and at herself for her behavior. She judged herself harshly.

"I acted like a seductress so I can't blame him for trying. If he thought I was easy, I deserved it." She fluctuated between feeling sorry for herself and blaming herself. She wasn't a tease, she wasn't a harlot, and yet here was someone who surely thought no more of her than that. Angry and hurt, she wasn't sure she didn't share his poor opinion of her. Why did she let him kiss her? Hadn't she earned his contempt? She had no right to have invited him to her apartment at such an hour. That she had willingly allowed herself to become involved in a compromising position was clear. It was, she decided at last, for the best. A man who was interested in her only to satisfy his lust was beneath her notice. And there was no reason to think of him at all. She had her career. She moved slowly into the kitchen where, with automatonlike stiffness, she poured the untouched drink down the drain and placed the uneaten cannolis in the trash. Curling up then on her living room sofa, she forced herself to think of other things. Like willing oneself to stop breathing, that was impossible.

CHAPTER V

Ten A.M. and the office was humming. The hollow ache in Bobbie's gut was beginning to abate. As soon as she had come into work, Larry had sailed passed Bobbie's desk, given her a meaningful look with his "Good morning," and winked, as though he were privy to state secrets. Bobbie had been ready to assure him that nothing had happened, but then figured that she wouldn't be believed anyway and it was hardly worth the trouble. Jerry remained studiously aloof, giving her only a barely perceptible nod as he passed with his coffee mug. Sure that he had already heard the news of the previous evening, Bobbie was not surprised when Cal Nesbitt greeted her heartily.

"Anything to report?" he asked in a voice lowered to a conspiratorial timbre.

"Cal, I think you'd better count me out of this."

"I thought we'd discussed it," he retorted sharply. Suddenly he turned on his heels. "I'll be in my office if you have to see me."

"What a crock!" Bobbie seethed inwardly. Men were all the same, whether in the office, the dance hall, or the marketplace. Well, nobody was going to boss her around, come hell or high water! She had let Dan Allen know that last night and she was going to let Cal Nesbitt know this morning. She marched resolutely into his office.

"Mr. Nesbitt—"

"Sit down, Bobbie."

"I prefer to stand, thank you. Mr. Nesbitt, when you hired me, it was as a cartoonist. I don't believe the word 'spy' entered into the job description. I'm doing what I was hired to do, and if you don't mind, I'm doing it well."

"You're right, Schaeffer," Nesbitt scowled. "You're damn good at cartooning, and if you weren't, I'd tell you where to go. I will say one thing though. Don't fall for the mayor and then let your personal bias show in your work. That's one thing I won't stand for, no matter how skilled you are."

"There's no chance of that happening." Bobbie smiled thinly. "Well, thanks for your time."

Seated at her own desk, Bobbie smiled grimly. Confronting Nesbitt had proved easier than she had thought. Taking out the galley proofs of a cartoon she had submitted several days ago, she surveyed them with satisfaction. It was going to run today and was of the quality she had come to expect of herself. Though cartoons fell in the netherland between art and craft, she was not of the ilk of cartoonist who cared to fight for respect from the art world. She understood her craft and she took pride in it. Art didn't have to convey a message, a feeling, a mood perhaps, but cartoons had to say something. They had to be terse and they had to be clear. Bobbie always felt very confident when she was working. It was a confidence that was expressed in her creations. And it was a confidence that did not spill out into the other spheres of her life. It was that very lack of confidence that put her into such a state of shock when she picked up the phone on her desk to hear Dan Allen's voice. Today was opening day of the baseball season and he was going to throw the first ball at the Wildcat Stadium. Would she like to come for the game?

"Did you forget about last night?" She felt her throat constrict, making it hard to speak.

"I want to make it up to you. I was a lout last night."

Relieved, Bobbie took a deep breath. "Baseball game, hmm? I see you believe in giving a girl advance notice."

"I hereby give you advance notice that I will request your company on the spur of the moment for at least the next fifty years."

"And what happens when I'm seventy-seven?" she chortled. "Will you have had your fill of me and throw me out with the trash?"

"Not at all. I like older women," he said, laughing.

"You're a hopeless flirt," she retorted.

"So how about the game? It's at two."

"All right. That is if I can get out of here in time."

"I have no doubt you'll manage. Call if you can't make it."

His faith in her was justified, for hardly was the morning over when Bobbie had the finishing touches on a cartoon depicting a three-ring circus: one ring was the political arena, the second was the media, and the third was the unions.

"There," she giggled to herself. "That ought to alienate just about everybody." Picking up the stoneware mug, she went down the hall for a well-earned coffee break. She was just reaching for the Cremora when Hermani's syrupy voice stopped her hand in midair.

"You're doing well on all fronts, dahlink. You have Nesbitt eating out of your hand, and Allen, hah, hah, eating out of— Well, I hate to think where. Toodle, dahlink. Enjoy your day. As only you can."

Bobbie gasped audibly. "Take that back, you vicious gossip-monger!"

Hermani, her eyes narrowed into slits, hissed through

clenched teeth, "You have succeeded well in convincing Nesbitt of your opinion of me."

"I never said anything to Nesbitt about you," Bobbie protested vainly, for Hermani, with a disdainful shake of her bleached mane, had already wiggled far down the corridor.

Her hand shaking so, Bobbie decided to forgo the coffee lest she spill it all over the floor. She felt as though she had been mugged! Hermani, with all the crassness she could muster, had impugned her morality and her ethics. Why in the world did she think she had said anything about her to the chief? And then she remembered Larry had told her that Nesbitt had called Hermani in to take her down a peg, after she had embarrassed Bobbie in front of the entire newsroom. Hermani probably thought Bobbie had complained about the incident. Bobbie fumed. As much as she detested the woman, Bobbie was not a carrier of tales. She would fight her own battles. The gall of that woman! She walked slowly back to her office and picked up her day's work to show Nesbitt. She hoped he would be pleased, for then she could ask, with a fair degree of impunity, for the rest of the day off.

As she knocked on Nesbitt's door she turned around, for she felt vaguely uncomfortable about something, only to meet Hermani's eyes shooting daggers at her. With a sinking feeling Bobbie realized what Hermani thought: Goody-Two-Shoes was going to tattle again! Bobbie feared that she was going to suffer heavy losses in any battle with Hermani.

Cal Nesbitt was in a receptive mood. He even laughed at Bobbie's cartoon.

"They can't accuse the press of bias if we knock ourselves in our own paper. I don't know if I agree with your judgment of the media, but it might make for good relations with the public. Make us look honest. We'll print it!"

"I'm glad you see it that way. I was a little worried," Bobbie admitted. She stood there awkwardly. Nesbitt looked up again, surprised. He was a man of few words, and after he said what he had to say, he expected his staff to leave.

"Anything else?" he scowled.

"Yes, sir. I was wondering— I mean, would you mind very much if I left early today?"

"Give 'em a hand, they take an arm," he barked. "I told you not to get used to half days. If you want to work part-time, I'll be glad to adjust your salary."

Bobbie nodded, swallowed hard, and practically ran out of his office.

This was a bad day, she thought. Maybe she should have stayed home in bed. Her chin in her hands, she sat immobile at her desk, just staring at the walls. She jumped in surprise when her door flew open and Nesbitt himself strode in with an armload of files. He raised his eyebrows but did not remark on her attitude.

"Look through these files on the housing project. See if you can get an angle on it for tomorrow. And after you're done, you can leave," he said blandly without looking in her direction.

"Thank you. I'll get right on it." Bobbie was touched by Nesbitt's capitulation to her request, though after she looked at the intricately detailed files he had left with her, she had the feeling she would be done in time for next year's opening game. Though it was with some reluctance that she opened the sheaf of papers, she found that she was absorbed in the mass of conflicting data regarding the housing project. She didn't know if she'd be able to untangle the web in order to arrive at the true facts and figures, but perhaps she could work around the idea of mass bureaucratic confusion—something to do with the right hand not knowing where the left was scratching.

58

When she looked at her watch, Bobbie was aghast to note that she had half an hour to make the game. She'd never make it. Better to call up the mayor's office with a message saying she'd be late. That way she could put these files in order and maybe even sneak some of them in her bag to work on at home that night. A strict rule of the office was that no information was to be removed without clearance, and she knew that this would never clear. It was still unsorted and it looked like there was some very juicy material to be found there. Bobbie dialed City Hall and dictated a message to the receptionist that she said was to be delivered to the mayor personally.

"I'm late for a very important date. Don't wait. Please leave my ticket at the main ticket office."

"The mayor's messages are picked up by his staff," the receptionist replied crisply, her tone clearly indicating that she thought Bobbie was not playing with a full deck.

"I'd appreciate it if you'd seal the note in an envelope, please, and ask whoever picks it up to give it to him. Thank you."

Bobbie cleared her desk, secreted in her outsize leather bag those papers that had particularly caught her interest, and returned the rest to Nesbitt's office, hoping that he would not notice that anything was missing. She was in luck; all he said as he took the bundle of papers was "Enjoy yourself and bring in the goods." Of course Bobbie hoped the goods he was referring to was her own work.

Driving in her usual maniacal style, Bobbie arrived at Wildcat Stadium at a little past three. She ran up to the main ticket office and was stunned to learn that no ticket was awaiting her.

"There must be a mistake," she insisted. "I'm with the mayor's party. He left a ticket for me."

"Sorry, ma'am. There's nothing here."

"Are you sure? Can't you look again?" she pleaded.

Looking at her with a mix of pity and exasperation, the man behind the iron cage obliged. He held up his hands. "Nothing."

"Well then, I will buy a ticket."

"Sold out. Sorry."

"If you'll let me go to him, I'm sure he will clear this up."

"Sorry. No ticket, no entry" was the terse reply.

"There must be something you can do!"

The man shook his head. "Opening day—sold out." Bobbie walked toward the parking lot, her shoulders hunched over dejectedly. Her mind was working over-time. She'd be damned if she'd just leave. To experience the zenith of emotion and the nadir in one day was not to her liking. It was marvelous to know that he regretted last night and hell to know that he'd forgotten her in the excitement of the new baseball season. There must be a mistake here and she was going to remedy it! But how? She couldn't sneak in, and heaven knows she was not going to scale concrete walls and climb in. She didn't have enough money to bribe her way in and she didn't have the clout to barge in. Suddenly she had it. Scouting out the grounds, she found a telephone booth out of sight of the ticket clerk. Not giving herself time to think about what she was doing, she inserted the coins and waited for an answer.

"All lines are temporarily busy. Please hold. Your call will be processed to the first available operator," the recording intoned. Bobbie was then obliged to listen to five minutes of Muzak, the last thing she wanted to do in her anxious state.

"Wildcat Stadium. Can I help you?"

"Good afternoon," Bobbie said in a nasal voice. "This is the White House calling. The President of the United States is waiting on the line for Mayor Dan Allen."

60

"The President of the United States?" the operator repeated, awe-struck.

"That's correct," Bobbie said, businesslike. "Will you have the mayor paged, please?"

"Yes, right away. Hold on!"

Bobbie fought the urge to break out in giggles. That poor operator sounded like she was going to burst! She didn't have more than five minutes to wait till her efforts were rewarded.

"Dan Allen speaking."

"Hello, Dan Allen," she cooed.

"Bobbie! What's this all about? Where are you?"

"In the parking lot, trying to get in to see you with a nonexistent ticket."

"I got a message saying you weren't coming."

"I never sent a message like that."

"Well, never mind. I'll have Coleman go up to the entrance with your ticket. By the way, that was a very clever stunt. I didn't know you had it in you."

"Were you disappointed that it was only me?"

"Not a chance. Mr. President doesn't set my heart a-throbbing."

Bobbie laughed. "See you in a minute." She felt like skipping as she hurried up to the stadium, past the bewildered ticket clerk, and to the wide doors at the entrance. Coleman was waiting for her, his face a study in irritation.

"Hi," Bobbie greeted him cheerily.

"Uh-huh," he responded.

Bobbie took the ticket he held out to her and handed it to the attendant. "What's the score?" she asked. Coleman shrugged. Bewildered by his lack of civility, his animosity, even, Bobbie lapsed into silence as she followed him all the way down to the mayor's box.

"Way to go! Atta boy," Dan was shouting as she approached, all propriety left behind as he got caught up in the game.

There were two other people in the mayor's party, whom she did not know, and, she was gratified to note, an empty chair to his right. Dan beamed as she squeezed over to her seat.

"Hello again, Lady of Many Resources. Pulled off any coups since I last spoke to you?"

"None at all." She smiled.

"Look at that, a sure double." Dan jumped to his feet. "Go, go." Bobbie grinned at him benignly. No one would guess, looking at him now, that this man was one of the most influential in the Midwest.

"Oh, no, that guy doesn't know what he's doing!" Dan exclaimed angrily as the umpire called the Wildcats runner out at second. "He was safe by a good foot. Ah!" He turned to Bobbie. "Sorry I didn't introduce you. This is C. J. Forstader, the owner of the Wildcats, and Sandra Wilkes, my attorney. You've met Elliot Coleman already."

Bobbie smiled and extended her hand to C. J. and Sandra. She was charmed by the former and taken sharply aback by the latter. A pang of jealousy hit her as she looked into Sandra's coolly appraising turquoise eyes. She was a raven-haired beauty with Slavic cheekbones, full-blown sensuous lips, and the bearing of a Greek goddess. Next to her Bobbie felt like a skinny, insipid mouse. And an attorney, no less! That meant she was brainy as well as beautiful. This was the sort of female any woman in her right mind would hasten to avoid. But it was for her that Dan was saving the seat next to him. Why? she asked herself tormentedly. As she tore her eyes away from Sandra, she noticed Coleman watching her with a small smile playing around the corners of his mouth.

"Dan"—Sandra leaned over, laying an alabaster hand

62

on his arm—"look at the way the outfield is playing Matthews to pull the ball. He should just tap it down the left-field line."

"Son of a gun, Sandra. You're right. We ought to have you out there instead of that clown of a manager. Do you see that, Bobbie?"

Bobbie shook her head. "How can you pull the ball? I thought you were supposed to hit it." As she noticed Dan's grimace she hastened to add, "I'm afraid the finer points of this game escape me. I just enjoy the action. And I like the hot dogs!" The approaching vendor smiled at that overhead remark.

"Coleman, get us five dogs. Mustard and sauerkraut?" Dan asked Bobbie.

"The works."

Everyone, with hot dog in hand, was eagerly watching the action on the diamond. Except Bobbie. She found it more interesting to observe the members of the mayor's party as they chomped on their hot dogs. Coleman munched on his, biting off little pieces; Forstader wolfed his down, finishing in two bites; Sandra looked alluring even when chewing; and Dan ate his absentmindedly, savoring each individual bite but appearing to forget about the spongy roll he pressed in his hand when the Wildcats were at bat. As for herself, Bobbie didn't know. She thought that one day when she had nothing to do she ought to eat in front of the mirror to see how she looked. Suddenly she was snapped out of her reverie as Dan jumped to his feet along with the rest of the stadium, for the Wildcats had just hit a grand slam in the bottom of the fifth inning, moving them ahead 4–2. Dan Allen, followed by the rest of the group, sat down with satisfaction written on his face.

"C.J."—Dan toasted the team's owner with the remainder of his hot dog—"congratulations." The worry lines on

C.J.'s prematurely wrinkled forehead smoothed out a bit as he settled complacently into his seat.

"This is an opportune time to bring up a business proposal, Dan," he drawled. "Are we among friends?"

"Feel free to talk," Dan said.

"Mayor!" Coleman warned with a nod in Bobbie's direction.

"Relax, Coleman. Bobbie's off duty now and she's okay. Go on, C.J."

"I'll be blunt, Dan. I want the city to forgive the back taxes we owe. The money, as you know, was used to renovate the stadium. A solid, attractive stadium draws revenue into Milwaukee, so you wouldn't lose anything. You'd be ahead of the game."

"I don't know, C.J. I'll have to think about it," Dan said doubtfully.

"I'm prepared to channel fifty grand into your reelection campaign through various sources," C.J. explained, pursuing his point.

"Fifty thousand, eh? That's above and beyond the legal limit."

"Don't worry, Dan. It'll wash. What do you say?" C.J. cracked his knuckles.

"Give me a day or two to check it out." Sandra whispered something into Dan's ear. He patted her hand. Bobbie winced visibly. She hated what she'd seen and she couldn't believe what she'd heard.

"Get the mayor," Cal Nesbitt had ordered her. "The end justifies the means," Machiavelli had written. Well, if she was sincerely committed to getting Mayor Allen out of office, and his party with him, she had the ammunition. C.J. was proposing illegal campaign contributions in return for an illegal forgiving of his debt to the city. What a scandal that would make! First rate! a small voice inside her head whispered, and how it would help her career to plant the first seeds of that scandal in a devastatingly funny cartoon. C.J., with his simian forehead and scrunched-up face, would be simple to caricature and unmistakably easy to identify. Best of all, a liberal mayor could soon take over the municipal government and undo all of the conservative measures that Mayor Allen had instituted. She looked up to meet once more Coleman's shrewd, unflinching gaze. It seemed to her that he was reading her mind. How she loathed that man!

With a toss of her head Bobbie put those demonic reflections where they belonged—nowhere. Never would she betray a confidence; she was here as a trusted friend. She wished it could be as much more, for she was beginning to feel an irresistible attraction and affection for Dan Allen, which was putting to the test all of her resolve not to involve herself in romantic entanglements. It was true that she woke up in the morning thinking of Dan Allen and that she went to sleep at night thinking of Dan Allen. She told herself over and over again to cease her silliness, for of course she wasn't his type. And his attentions to her were meaningless. He acted that way to all women. But there was always that faint hope shimmering inside her that she would be a modern-day Cinderella. *Stop dreaming!* she scolded herself silently. *You're no match for Sandra, and to boot, she even talks baseballese.*

"Would you all like to view the rest of the game over a drink from my indoor box?" C.J. addressed the group.

"That sounds good," Dan agreed. He looked inquiringly at the others, who assented with nods and murmurs. As the group rose to walk up to the ultramodern glass enclosure, C.J. waited for Dan to step in the aisle, where he then proceeded, in a much lower tone, to bend Dan's ear about something or other. Coleman took Sandra's arm and spoke to her rapidly in a staccato voice. Sandra's eyes shot daggers as she looked back at Bobbie, but Coleman expertly brought her attention to him with a whispered phrase. That left Bobbie to bring up a solitary rear, feeling the target of misdirected animosity as well as the proverbial fifth wheel. Flashbulbs popped in her face once or twice, almost making her stumble on the steep concrete stairs. Bobbie didn't know how Dan stood the flood of celebrity-seekers constantly hounding him with their cameras and their pleas for his autograph. Being a mayor—well, a handsome, glamorous mayor—was as bad as being a movie star! Whoever had taken her picture would be sorry when they found out that she was an unknown.

The owner's box was lined in plush red velvet. Sinking gratefully into a soft armchair, Bobbie thought that this was the way to watch a baseball game. The plate-glass window in front of them was so clean, it was almost invisible. It was with such glee that C.J. displayed his gadgetry: the headphones with the dials that brought in every TV and radio station of any importance across the nation that was running the game; and the computer printout with batting averages and earned-run averages, which reminded Bobbie of the adage that little boys never grow up, they just grow older.

With the game's end Dan announced that all the excitement had given him an appetite. It was giving Bobbie a headache.

"How about everybody coming over to my place for spaghetti?" Dan asked.

"Did you say what I think you said?" Sandra chortled. "*You're* going to cook for us? Or are you planning on having it catered?"

"Even I can open a jar of spaghetti sauce," Dan said good-naturedly. "Let's all forget that this is the mayor, okay? Everybody's invited! You too, dear," he addressed the buxom, red-haired secretary who had hastened over at

C.J.'s bidding to take a quickly dictated note to the Wildcats' manager.

"Why, thank you, Mayor. I'd be delighted," she gushed.

"My pleasure." He winked at her, then leaned across Coleman to ask Bobbie if anything was wrong. She was so quiet.

"I'm fine. Enjoying the scenery." She smiled through her misery. She didn't know what else to say. For the first time since grade school she was utterly tongue-tied. There was no rhyme nor reason for her presence here. No one, least of all Dan, had paid her much mind and now she was going to be stuck accepting his dinner invitation. She knew now, for a fact, that this invitation, along with all his others, meant nothing. He liked to be surrounded by people, especially women. Hadn't he just invited that simpering secretary to his house also? Having lost sight of the fact that he was a politician through and through had been her undoing. Before they could even run for office, politicians had to get a degree in charm, and Dan's had been a Ph.D. Bobbie bit her lip. Never had she thought she would end up a political groupie!

"You're my kind of guy!" C.J. exclaimed jovially. "Tell you what I'll do. They've got some bottles of my favorite red stashed away for me here. That will be my contribution." He beckoned to the waiter and told him to wrap up four bottles of the Zifandel '70. "Shall we take my car?"

"I have my limo and my driver waiting," Dan offered. "That might be more comfortable."

"Nothing is more comfortable than my Mercedes," C.J. boasted.

"We'll meet you at my house then. You have the address?"

"Sure thing. You come with me, pussycat," he ordered his secretary.

That poor girl! Bobbie thought with wry humor. *Dan calls her dear; C.J. calls her Pussycat. I guess her mother forgot to name her!*

"Dan, I think I am going to have to beg out of this one. I have work to do at home," Bobbie said halfheartedly.

"Nonsense! I need someone to serve drinks." His eyes twinkled with the reference to the incident at her apartment.

On the ride there Bobbie regretted that she had been so easily convinced, for once more she was left out of the conversation. Sandra was filling Dan in on a legal matter to come before the City Council, and Coleman, taciturn and dour, looked straight ahead. Somehow the dinner conversation wasn't quite right either. It didn't jell. There was a good deal of talking going on, but it seemed to her that there was fearful little communication to go with it. The best part of the day so far was in the kitchen when Dan had asked her to prepare the garlic bread. It was nice working at the counter next to him; it gave her a homey, warm feeling. Now, as she wound the perfectly al dente strands of spaghetti around her fork, she wished that the evening would end. The others may have felt the strain as well, for there seemed to be unanimous agreement that the press of time meant that cordials would have to be skipped. Bobbie guessed that everyone, even C.J., was in awe of Dan Allen and a little nervous when left holding the conversational bag.

"Are you going back to the stadium?" Bobbie asked C.J. "My car is there."

"I'll drive you later," Dan interrupted before C.J. could answer.

Bobbie gulped. "I don't want to put you to any trouble." She promptly felt like kicking herself. What a dumb thing to say.

"That's the kind of trouble I like," Dan murmured.

68

C.J. left with a fraternal punch in the arm for Dan and a wave for Bobbie. His secretary tittered her good-bye. Sandra left with a bright smile for Dan and a condescending nod in Bobbie's direction. Coleman harrumphed without looking at either one of them.

"I'm glad that ordeal is over," Dan said as he closed the door.

"You seemed to be enjoying yourself," Bobbie commented dryly.

"Don't let the role I'm playing fool you."

"Maybe you're in the wrong profession then."

"Not at all," Dan corrected her. "We both know I'm excellent at what I do. Milwaukee has never been in better shape. My beliefs are strong and I'm one of the few who can say their campaign promises are their policies. It's just that I prefer not to be 'on' twenty-four hours a day."

"Is tooting your own horn one of your beliefs?"

"Hey," he said gently, "what's the matter?"

"You know I'm one hundred percent opposed to your politics. We couldn't be farther apart in terms of ideology. I believe in subsidized housing and day-care centers for the poor. You don't. I believe in affirmative-action programs for women and minorities in jobs and education. You don't. The list is endless. We're like oil and water, and we really shouldn't be trying to mix. That is, I shouldn't be trying. I don't know what *your* game is."

Dan touched his finger to her lips. "A. Politics is *verboten* here. Neither of us is going to change and I prefer not to quarrel about it. B. What in hell are you talking about? My game, simply stated, is Hearts. I'm wearing mine on my sleeve."

"Are you, Dan?"

"Let me kiss you, and then you tell me whether I'm lying."

"I'll clear the table for you," she said falteringly. She

69

quickly turned her back and busied herself so Dan couldn't see her cheeks flush in embarrassment.

"Don't bother. The girl will come in tomorrow morning."

"I'll just put the dishes in the sink. You'll feel better with this mess cleared up, you'll see." She went about carrying plates and glasses from the dining room to the country-style kitchen. She trod gingerly, so as not to drop anything on the exquisite Oriental rug that covered the walnut parquet floors of the Chinese-motif dining room. Dan leaned lazily against the black lacquered sideboard with its antique lamp, jade figurines, and ceramic vases. His arms were folded across his chest and his smile was indolent as he watched Bobbie rushing to and fro between the rooms.

"You look kind of sweet in that wifely attitude," he joked.

"It's more like a maid than a wife," she said liltingly.

"They're not all that different."

"No wonder you're not married," she snapped. "And it's a good thing I'm finished, because after that comment I'd simply have to refuse, in the name of womanhood, you know, to do any more."

"Oh-ho-ho. Now I know how to get a rise out of you."

"You haven't had much trouble in that respect."

"You're cute when you're angry."

"Oh, that's original. Do you need all your advanced degrees in political science to think up lines like that?"

"You've got a quick temper," he said with amusement.

"You've got a quicker tongue," she flashed.

"I haven't heard you say this much all day. I thought you'd lost your voice."

"Your friends aren't the most easygoing people in the world," she said matter-of-factly.

"You're using the word 'friend' rather too loosely. Associates would be more appropriate. Coleman's a first-rate aide, but I don't know that I would want to go on a fishing trip with him. And C.J.—well, he's a businessman. That's a different breed altogether. If I were voted out of office tomorrow and became an insurance salesman, I doubt that he'd remember my name."

"What about Sandra?" Bobbie asked despite all reason.

"Sandra"—his voice softened—"is a damn good lawyer and a friend."

"Oh," Bobbie said in a small voice.

"Now we come to you," Dan said smoothly.

"I'm just your friendly neighborhood media person," Bobbie said in a light tone that she hoped concealed the turmoil in her heart.

"You're my friend too, I think." He looked questioningly at Bobbie.

"Of course I am!" she said jovially.

"But you're also more than that. I think about you when I'm not with you. When I'm in meetings, when I'm reviewing legislation, there's your face popping up in front of me. You're a damn nuisance, that's what!" he ended on a light note.

"I'll try to keep my face where it belongs," she assured him with mock-gravity.

"Would you think it crazy if I said I was falling in love with you?" he pursued.

"Not crazy," she teased, "just a little weird." She tried to remain relaxed, though she could feel her pulse exceeding its aerobic maximum.

"Perhaps I'm taking this whole thing too seriously," Dan said soberly.

"No, no." Bobbie moved closer to him, her head tilted back and her lips half-parted.

"I accept the invitation," Dan murmured as he bent to kiss her.

71

As soon as his lips met hers this second time, she knew she belonged to him. All the hurt seemed to melt with the sweetness of his kiss. He covered her face, the long golden column of her neck, and the delicate, ivory lobes of her ears with his kisses. His hands followed the path his searing lips blazed down her shoulders to the provocative fullness of her breasts.

Hardly able to restrain a moan as she felt his hot breath through the thin silk of her blouse, first upon one nipple and then the other, she leaned against him, allowing his strength to support her. Running her fingers through his thick black curly hair, she held him to her, wanting to stop these moments in time.

As he thrust his hard body against her, they became locked in an embrace both magical and passionate. Holding tight, they sank slowly to the thick cream rug with its pattern of fire-breathing dragons and covered bridges. As she stretched out beside him she felt an urgency of desire that made her gasp. Dan raised himself on one elbow and smiled down at her. With measured slowness he unbuttoned her blouse and unfastened her bra. Sweeping the garments off her, he contemplated the vision before him. His hands cupped the swelling mounds as he watched the nipples harden obediently under his touch. She held her slender arms up to his neck. As she saw the hunger in his eyes, with its mix of passion and admiration, she wanted to open herself to this man as she had never opened herself to anyone before.

"Oh, Dan, I want you to make love to me. I want you."

"You'll have me, my sweet, in good time. First I want to revel in the sight of you." With one deft movement he unzipped her velvet jeans and pulled them off along with her bikini panties. His hands freely roamed her lush naked body. Though he was fully dressed, Bobbie felt no shame. Modesty and inhibition were words that she had always

72

lived with but that she forgot now in her desire to give him pleasure. With his eyes never leaving her, he stood to undress. Just then the phone rang. Dan excused himself to answer it.

"Why, hello," she heard him say warmly from the next room.

"Nothing special," he answered to an unknown query. He lowered his voice then and all she heard was his short laugh and murmurings. Goose bumps appeared on her arms and she felt suddenly cold. Curling her legs up, she strained her ears to overhear him say with exasperation, "Sandra, we've discussed that before. Can't it wait till tomorrow? I have company." He paused, then said acerbically, "You are annoying me. I don't want to talk about it now."

As though a light bulb clicked on in her mind, Bobbie grabbed for her clothes. What was she doing here lying naked on the floor and he practically advertising the fact? She must be out of her mind. And what kind of gall did he have to leave her there while he spoke to his lawyer? Lawyer, hah! More like his mistress. Maybe she had a law degree, maybe she didn't. But as his attorney he could keep her on his payroll at the public expense. She knew how things like that worked. She was a newspaperperson, wasn't she? Thank heaven for that phone call that had brought her to her senses. Dan Allen had a way with words and he was used to getting what he wanted. He had taken a fancy to her and, had the fates not intervened, would have had his way with her. She was just belting her coat in the living room as he returned, a bewildered expression on his face.

"Where are you going?"

"Home, Dan."

"Are you angry because I was talking on the phone? I'm sorry, but it was an important matter. In my line of work

73

I can't punch out at five o'clock. Take off your coat and sit down."

"Nothing further will be taken off at your request," she retorted scathingly. "And please save your excuses. I am not interested. Although"—she hesitated—"it didn't sound like municipal matters you were discussing!"

"Why must you make things so difficult?" he sighed.

"You won't have to worry about that anymore."

"You're a pussycat," he said huskily.

"I'm a scorpion," she scoffed. "And scorpions eat their mates. So be glad you're rid of me. Don't worry about driving me home."

"But you don't have your car here. At least let me call you a cab."

"No, I'll manage," she said sharply. "I'm a big girl."

"You think you are," he said resignedly. "Thanks for cleaning up."

"I'll send you my bill in the morning," she snapped as she slammed the door behind her.

The cool night air slapped her cheeks and cleared her mind as she walked to first one bus stop and then another. It was better to keep moving. The pale moon lent an eerie beauty to the wide boulevard with its stone mansions and well-trimmed hedges. The world was a varied place. She had eyes for seeing and ears for hearing. She had a good mind. She didn't need anything or anyone else. With or without Dan Allen she could gaze at the moon and smell the first buds of spring. With firm resolve she knew that he would never make a fool of her again. Before she knew it, so lost in thought was she, she was home, having walked all the way. It had taken longer than she had expected, for as she unlocked her door the church bells rang out eleven times. Suddenly she remembered she had forgotten to pick up her car at the stadium. Too tired to do anything now, she decided to worry about that tomorrow. Without changing into her nightgown, Bobbie flopped across her bed and fell into a heavy sleep. Her last thought before losing consciousness was that she'd probably be late for work tomorrow. Somehow she just didn't care.

CHAPTER VI

Not only did Bobbie oversleep the next morning, she skipped work altogether. Having been awakened at three in the morning by the phone ringing, she had lain there until five before she fell asleep again. The call must have been a wrong number, for, after hearing her sleepy hello, the caller had hung up.

Glancing in her mirror that morning, Bobbie had the urge to cover it. She saw reflected in the glass a young woman with mascara smeared around her eyes and old lipstick on her mouth. Granted, the woman was attractive, almost unrecognizably so, with her chic hairdo and even with her stale makeup, but she wasn't Bobbie. In the shower she scrubbed her face, washed and towel-dried her hair, and pulled it back in one severe braid. She put away the soft contact lenses she had worn last night and donned her glasses. After pulling on a pair of brown corduroy jeans and a white shirt, she surveyed herself anew. The natural look did nothing to soften the planes of her face, and the glasses hid her long lashes; her unisex clothes made her appear a bit angular, but happily she recognized herself. *This* was Bobbie Schaeffer. And Bobbie Schaeffer ought to be at work. But Nesbitt had a backlog of good cartoons, any one of which he could run since they dealt with ongoing topics. A day at home was something she felt she owed herself since she had never once called in sick.

Little did she know herself. Even though she had looked forward to reading a new mystery novel, so imbued with the work ethic was she that she spent a good deal of her time wondering what was going on at the office. And she spent a good deal of time wondering whether she had been too hasty in leaving Dan's last night. After all, he wasn't the one who made the call to Sandra. He had only answered, and from what she had overheard, he hadn't been overly friendly to her.

A heavy rapping on her door made Bobbie jump. Cautiously peeping out with chain still locked, Bobbie was flabbergasted to see a messenger in uniform hidden behind an enormous bouquet of yellow roses.

"Are those for me?" Bobbie asked incredulously. "How many are there?"

"Four dozen, ma'am."

"They're beautiful, just breathtaking."

"Yes, ma'am. Do you want me to bring them in?"

"Of course. I'm sorry." She hastily unchained the lock and ushered the messenger into the living room. "You can lay them on the table over there."

"Fine. You'll have to sign for these, ma'am." He took a pencil from behind his ear and held out a receipt book to Bobbie. She was scribbling her name next to the X when her glance happened to fall on the top line. The name Sandra Wilkes and an address on the west side of town were clearly printed there.

"I'm afraid you've made a mistake. These flowers are supposed to go to Sandra Wilkes." Her words came out in a high-pitched shriek. "Please take them to her."

"Listen, lady, I've been there and she told me to bring the flowers here. I've got a truck full of flowers to deliver. I can't be goin' on a wild goose chase from the west side of town to the east and then back again. No, ma'am, I'm sorry but I've done my part."

Bobbie nodded mutely and turned to the flowers, where she searched for the card that would solve this mystery. It was what she had feared. The note was short, written in Dan Allen's hand.

Sandra,
Sorry if I was abrupt with you last night. You do understand. Thanks for everything.

Dan.

A rage welled up in Bobbie's breast that made her glad she was a nonviolent person.

"You all right, ma'am?" It was the messenger speaking.

Bobbie looked up to see him hovering reluctantly near the door. It occurred to her that he was waiting for a tip. She groped for her purse, pulled out a crumpled dollar bill, and handed it to him.

"Thanks. Enjoy the blossoms. They're mighty pretty." He closed the door behind him.

Of all the dirty tricks, Bobbie thought, this was a prize winner. She didn't know quite what Sandra was trying to prove, but whatever it was, she didn't like it. That Sandra was jealous, spiteful, and possessed little class was obvious. What was less clear was her reason. Did she want Bobbie to think that Dan was smitten with Sandra and that they were involved in some sort of secret affair? Did she want Bobbie to feel that Dan was a two-timer? Whatever her reasoning, this episode reflected more on Sandra than on Dan. The note was vague; it could mean many things, and Bobbie was darned if she was going to torment herself with it as Sandra had obviously hoped. She picked up the huge bouquet—Bobbie had never held so many roses—and went with them to the trash bins in the alley-way. She was about to drop them in with the refuse there when she felt a twinge of conscience. It would be a shame to throw them out. If she couldn't enjoy them, let someone else do so. She thought she could just drive them over to the old age home. All of a sudden she remembered she had left her car at the stadium. Grudgingly she went into the house and called a cab to take her to pick up the car. She was sure the driver shot her strange looks as she sat in the backseat with four dozen yellow roses on her lap. The Wildcats' parking lot attendant eyed her quizzically too, but then she flashed him a genuine smile and he seemed to understand. She was grateful when she finally got into the car, and headed straight for the old-age home she regularly passed on her way home from work.

The manager there was ever so grateful for the gift, showering her with blessings as she left the barely opened dewy buds at the main desk. She felt a twinge of conscience for accepting praise that she did not richly deserve. She herself wouldn't be able to stand the sight of those roses in her home and she feared that she would never be able to enjoy another yellow rose.

As she drove home Bobbie made a promise to herself. She would never mention the roses to Dan, even if by chance she did wind up speaking to him again. She would not bring herself down to Sandra's level.

When finally the day had passed and the new one arrived, Bobbie found herself at work with the janitorial staff. It was odd poring over the papers that had piled up in her absence, working with only the hum of vacuum cleaners in the background rather than the hustle and bustle of the busy newsroom. She read the previous day's *Post* carefully. They had run one of her consumer-oriented cartoons mocking the food-additive industry. It was an effective cartoon, she noted with satisfaction. A street vendor was handing a customer a hot dog and balancing mustard and ketchup in the other hand. He was asking if the man wanted some monosodium glutamate or red dye number two with his nitrates.

When finally she got to the People section of the paper, she sat openmouthed in horror. Swallowing hard, she read the caption under the picture of C.J. and Dan.

C. J. FORSTADER COZIES UP TO MIL-WAUKEE'S MAYOR. We're wondering if the beatitude of his expression had something to do with the erasure of his tax debt to the city, which those in the know say he's working successfully to achieve.

How could anyone from the *Post* have found out about that? There were only five people present at that conversation: C.J. himself, Dan, Coleman, Sandra, and herself. It was inconceivable that any of them could have broken the story.

Bobbie was furious with Cal Nesbitt. Of course the *Post* was opposed to Mayor Dan Allen on principle, but the implications concerning him in those two sentences were positively unethical. They made it sound as if Dan were a flunky for Forstader, and he was nothing of the kind. He hadn't made any promises, and knowing him, Bobbie doubted very much that he would. Her phone flashed. She picked it up.

"Good morning. I tried you at home, so I figured you were off to a good start at work."

"Good morning, Mayor," Bobbie said frostily.

"Don't get huffy with me. This isn't a social call. Why did you leak that story?"

Bobbie nearly choked. "I—I did nothing of the kind," she stammered.

"It's bad enough that you're an informer, a plant, or whatever nasty word one cares to use. But don't compound it by lying as well!"

"I swear to you," Bobbie gasped, "I— It wasn't me."

"I guess I owe you an apology then for a false accusation." Dan sounded mollified. "But you *are* the obvious suspect. Maybe someone planted a hidden tape recorder on you."

"Yes, in my false teeth," Bobbie replied in a lighter tone, hoping to placate him.

"This isn't a joking matter. It's quite serious. And I mean to get to the bottom of it. I want to believe you. But everyone who heard that conversation except for you has the best motive in the world—their own hides—to keep it quiet. If I go, Coleman and Sandra are out of jobs and C.J. is left holding not only the tab he owes but a charge of attempted bribery. Of course nothing can be proved. But charges, hints, these all leave a bad taste."

"You forgot the most important thing. You didn't accept C.J.'s offer," she pointed out.

"I know that. I'm not worried. My record speaks for itself. But if there's a Judas close to me, I want to know it. The worst poison is suspicion."

"I hope that poison is no longer directed against me," she said crisply.

"You have your own brand that you've been aiming in my direction, lady."

"I don't want to talk about it. Let's just sign off on friendly terms, okay?"

"There's no one friendlier than I," Dan agreed. "See you around, kid." Without giving Bobbie the opportunity to respond, he clicked off, leaving her cradling the phone in puzzlement.

Well, so much for him! Bobbie thought for the thousandth time. Burying herself in the ticker-tape piled on her desk after perusing the sports and real estate sections of the paper, Bobbie tried vainly to think up a clever cartoon. All her ideas today seemed either too abstract or hack-

81

neyed. That was the trouble with holding a "creative" job. You couldn't wait for inspiration from your muse, but you had to turn it on like a water faucet. With this double mess about the mayor weighing on her mind she doubted that she could even get a trickle.

She shouldn't have even bothered trying, she thought, for things went from terrible to disastrous. Less than an hour after Dan's call there was a sharp rapping at her door. Without even waiting for an acknowledgment, Elliot Coleman barged in, his face twisted with fury.

"Schaeffer, we've got words for broads like you and none of them are flattering. I want you to march right into your editor's office and tell him you fabricated that story. Otherwise I'll make a couple of well-placed calls and you'll be peddling your comics on the street corner!" he sneered.

"Get out!" Bobbie jumped to her feet, shouting with her finger pointing to the door. "Don't you dare ever threaten me again! And for the record I'm innocent and I don't care whether you believe that!" If she didn't care, why did she even bother telling him? she mentally berated herself.

"Our mayor may be a sucker for you, but don't try the same thing with me. And while I'm at it, I'll tell you this: I don't want you to see him again. Someone like you can ruin him, which is probably what you want in the first place. I'll give you a last word of advice: *Take* my advice." With that ultimatum Coleman spun on his heel, military style, and stalked out of her office.

Her temples pounding, Bobbie felt like rushing after him and decking him. Instead she stood there gripping the edge of her desk, not sure whether she was going to cry, scream, or eat a six-pack of Hershey bars. Coleman was not worth her time, she tried vainly to convince herself. His only redeeming quality was his association with Dan. She supposed that was why his words hurt. He had most likely expressed the same sentiments to Dan, which may have prompted Dan's phone call that morning. That would mean that some part of Dan, at least, had agreed with Coleman.

Bobbie paced up and down her small office, trying to figure out who could have leaked the story. No matter how she figured it, she laughed sardonically, she came up with only one possible answer: She was the guilty one. But of course she wasn't—not unless she walked, dialed, and talked in her sleep. In disgust she sat down to get some work done. Her mind, however, refused to obey her, wandering at will to the unpleasant subject. Since she wasn't going to produce very much that would be worthwhile, she decided to seek out some pleasant company. Her ego needed it. She headed for Jerry's office. Just as she turned the corner whom should she see but Coleman and, of all people, Hermani deep in conversation. Clutching her side, she turned back again, desperate to avoid a confrontation with her two least favorite people. She may have been too late, for Hermani's voice, tinged with malice, tinkled down the hallway. "Why do you think he hired her in the first place, dahlink?" Coleman's whispered answer made Hermani laugh as if her sides were splitting. Five minutes passed and Bobbie was relieved to note that the winsome pair had disappeared. She walked quickly to Jerry's office.

"Hey," he beamed, "where have you been hiding? I've missed you the last week or so. There's not so many willing ears I can complain to around here."

"So that's what I am," she teased. "A willing ear."

"Let me elaborate on that point. You are my friend and my willing ear."

"Those kind words are music to *my* ears, to coin a cliché. You have no idea what a morning I've had." She slumped into the hard-backed chair across from him.

"Let me get you a cup of coffee and you can tell me all

83

about it," he said solicitously. Jerry was better than his word. He came back with the coffee and a cherry tart.

"Where did you get that?" she queried.

"Connections." He laughed. "You look like you need something to cheer you up. So tell Papa Jerry. What's the problem? No, drink your coffee first and eat," he amended. He watched her as she took a big bite of the custard-filled confection.

"Mmmm, this is nirvana," she said. "Want a bite?"

"You better believe it!" With that he took a bite that left Bobbie holding at most a square inch of the tart.

"So much for generosity," she groaned.

He laughed. "What a creep I am. Tell you what. That dastardly move calls for penance. I'm taking you out to lunch." He glanced at his watch. "It's eleven thirty. This way we can beat the noon crowds."

"That's all right with me. I could use some pampering."

"Pampering coming up. I'm taking you to the Etoile," he stated, referring to Milwaukee's finest French restaurant.

"Are you sure you can afford it?" she asked doubtfully. "The corner hot dog stand would do just as well. All that's important is a friendly face."

He held up his hands in a gesture of protest. "C'mon. No time to waste." He drove at breakneck speed to Whitefish Bay, a posh suburb of Milwaukee, where the Etoile was located in an old converted town house.

The ambience of the restaurant was understated yet expensive. Toulouse-Lautrec lithographs lined the wall, and the Tiffany lamps, which provided the illumination even at midday, were turn of the century. The china was Limoges and the silverware was real silver, Bobbie noted as the maître d' seated them.

"My gosh, Jerry, I didn't know you frequented this sort of restaurant."

"To tell you the truth, this is my first time here," he admitted.

"We can still leave," Bobbie pointed out. "This place is going to cost a fortune."

"Please, I want to eat here with you. Did I tell you my new philosophy about money? No? Well, you know I was the last of the great savers, and then one day I looked in my bank book and there was, to my standards, an enormous sum there. I felt great. But then I got to thinking about what I'd been doing with my life. And I thought of all the crumpled, old, reused brown bags I was lugging to work, the little pieces of aluminum foil I used to rinse off, the Hamburger Helper I used so often to stretch the meat, and I realized that all I had to show for my life was a drawer full of coupons and bits of string. I was stingy with money and I was stingy with myself. I wasn't living. Well, all that's changed now, and I want you to be one of the first to know. And," he guffawed, "I'm going to tell you as soon as you get your problems off your chest."

"Oh, no, you don't," Bobbie protested vehemently. "I refuse to be left hanging. This is your story. You started, so you finish. And it sounds like a happy tale, which is just what I need to hear."

"If you insist," Jerry conceded, smiling. "To make a long story short, I'm a new man. Living life to the fullest and—you'll never believe this—"

"Let me guess," Bobbie broke in laughingly. "You're having a baby!"

"You're close," Jerry bantered as he tweaked her nose. "I'm in love."

"You're in love," Bobbie repeated. "That's wonderful! And who's the lucky girl?"

"Larry." Jerry smiled diffidently.

"Larry!" Bobbie gulped. "I didn't know. Well, congratulations!" Bobbie bit her lip and concentrated on act-ing blasé. She had always known about Larry. He made it obvious. But Jerry! She never would have dreamed that he was that way! Of course she couldn't care less, she thought. Larry and Jerry were her friends, and what they did together was their business.

"Larry is energetic, honest, and open—the opposite of secretive, matter-of-fact me." Jerry folded his arms on the table. "He's made me see what I was missing. It's as if I was born blind and suddenly given my sight. The whole world looks different. He's taught me to see and he's taught me that I can eat filet of sole *meunière* for lunch instead of bologna and cheese. He's also taught me that friendships are worth nurturing and that pennies or even big bucks shouldn't be allowed to stand between people."

"Whew! What a testimonial!" Bobbie smiled. "I'll bet if Larry heard you, he'd crawl under the table. Tell me, how come I didn't know about this the night of the Pabst Theatre Ball? Were you guys so secretive about it?"

"I think you weren't looking," Jerry answered. "Your attention was directed elsewhere."

"So it was," Bobbie conceded glumly as the image of Dan's face danced before her eyes. She could almost feel the rough texture of his skin and hear the caressing tones of his voice. She was brought back to earth by Jerry tapping her on the arm.

"Jerry calling Bobbie. Come in, Bobbie, over and out."

"Oh, sorry," she apologized, returning her attention to him. "Why don't we skip my part of this conversation? I don't want to ruin the levity of this outing."

"A deal's a deal," Jerry frowned. "Look, even though I've got a new outlook, if you don't get this all off your chest, there's no way—Larry or no Larry—that I can justify this lunch. How's that for manipulation?" He grinned.

"Not bad. You could write the book." Bobbie laughed resignedly. "Okay, I'll tell you, but only on one condition."

"What's that?"

"You must promise to forget what I've told you right afterward and must swear not to divulge one word of it to anybody, except maybe Larry."

"I won't make any guarantees about my memory or lack of it, but I do swear silence. You can count on it."

"This could be a good story for you," Bobbie said doubtfully. She was having second thoughts about confiding in a newspaperman.

"A journalist is only as good as his word," Jerry reassured her. Just then the waiter came over to take their order. True to his word, Jerry ordered the filet of sole, and Bobbie, conscious of her waistline and Jerry's budget, despite his disclaimers, ordered a spinach salad and a glass of white wine.

"All right, Jerry. Here goes." She talked nonstop for twenty minutes, her final sentence coinciding with the arrival of lunch.

"How's that for a tale of woe?" she asked mournfully.

"It's another Madame Butterfly," he answered sympathetically. "Do you have any idea how that story could have appeared?"

"None. There's no reason why anybody there should have leaked it."

"Maybe someone else overheard the conversation," he suggested.

Bobbie nixed the idea. "That would have been impossible. One, the owner's box is pretty well isolated, and two, there was so much noise around, I could barely hear what was being said."

Jerry was thoughtful. "Let me check around. There's

got to be a motive involving one of the three people left: Coleman, C.J., or Sandra."

"It's not necessary. Really. I just wanted to get it off my chest, I didn't want you to get involved."

"Don't worry. I'll be discreet," Jerry said, rightfully guessing Bobbie's major concern. He almost cracked with laughter. "Let's enjoy the food." He dug into his fish with gusto. Bobbie picked at her salad, loath to tell him that at these prices the spinach leaves were sandy.

"Bobbie," he said as he wiped his mouth with the linen napkin, "you've got a fight on your hands. But we're going to get to the bottom of this, and I'm going to see you as Mrs. Mayor."

"Wait a minute!" she guffawed. "I don't want to be Mrs. anybody. I simply don't want my name besmirched."

"You're not fooling me. I know lovesick when I see it. And a good thing it is. Otherwise you'd end up old and bent with nothing but a scrapbook of cartoons, maybe a few awards, and nobody to show them to who really cared."

"You sound like my grandmother," she teased.

"Then you should listen to your grandmother."

"I'm perfectly happy with my life," Bobbie insisted. "I can take care of myself very well. I've got a career that I love."

"But does your career love you?" Jerry asked, wearing a profound expression.

"Now, what in the world is that supposed to mean?"

"Think about it, babe," Jerry hinted mysteriously.

"What I don't understand," Bobbie said slowly, "is why Hermani has taken such a dislike to me. I've never done anything to her." Jerry grimaced.

"That's an easy one. You're young, good-looking, and free. Hermani's just had her third face-lift and probably her hundredth rejection. She can't even pay for love anymore."

"I thought she was looking a little different lately," Bobbie teased. "She doesn't have two chins anymore—just two faces!"

CHAPTER VII

Jerry was as good as his word. The next day he strolled into Bobbie's office with a smug expression on his face and a small manila envelope under his arm.

"I did a lot of checking, but this is all I could find," he said as he tossed the envelope onto her desk and sat down. Bobbie took out the yellowed clippings.

"You really did do research," she said admiringly as she read the name of the now-defunct student gazette emblazoned across the top of the first bunch of clippings. As she studied the picture in the first clipping, Coleman's face jumped out at her from the group scene. It was a much younger-looking Coleman and, if it could be imagined, a more straitlaced and grimmer Coleman.

"No fraternity brother, this." Bobbie laughed dryly. Her eyebrows became knit as she read the articles. "The mayor can't know that he was a member of this organization! These people are nuts! And I thought he was conservative now!"

Jerry nodded thoughtfully. "From what I saw of him at the ball, Coleman is a man possessed with one single purpose: power. And as the mayor's right-hand man he would be understandably miffed if he saw you as a threat to the mayor."

"How could I be a threat? Let's face it, a half-dozen

cartoons do not a Jules Feiffer make. Barbara Walters isn't running to Milwaukee to interview me."

"No," Jerry contradicted her, "Coleman doesn't see you as a threat because of your position on the paper. I think it's because he saw the same thing that night of the ball that Larry and I saw."

"What's that?" Bobbie queried.

"A look of sublime love in the mayor's eyes whenever his glance rested upon you."

"Oh, cut it out!" Bobbie dismissed the comment with a wave of her hand.

"It's true. And *voilà* the threat. You no longer have a politician with nothing but politics on his mind. Everyone knows what a lot of energy politics takes. If Dan Allen's career plummets, Coleman's goes along with it. He can't afford a moonstruck boss. He would much prefer to keep the mayor footloose and fancy free and happy with a string of floozies."

"That's very flattering but equally removed from reality, I'm afraid," Bobbie said mournfully. "Dan Allen is much too level-headed to ever be carried away, and even if he weren't, I could never be the one to do it. I was simply a curiosity for our dear mayor, and although it embarrasses me to admit it, all he actually did when we went out to eat was to pump me and to cajole me into changing my mind about him. He is very image conscious, so Coleman doesn't have to worry."

"Your modesty is appealing, terribly feminine." Jerry smiled. "I won't argue with you about it, but let me continue with my hypothesis. Besides Coleman worrying about his boss's attention span in the dog-eat-dog political world, he doesn't want him going off and getting married —even if the mayor, fat and content, with a wife waiting for him in the kitchen at night, would double his involvement in politics after the nuptials were over. Why? Simple," he answered his own rhetorical question. "Look around you. Who are the hottest politicians in the country? The handsome, glamorous, dedicated bachelors. And I'll bet you that one of them will soon be president. I have a gut feeling that Coleman's political aspirations don't end in Milwaukee. I rest my case."

"What are you saying? That Coleman planted that piece in the paper to frame me?"

"It's a possibility, isn't it? You saw that photograph of him in college. That's the look of a fanatic. People don't change that much, even if they try to change. I can tell you about that. I tried hard enough."

Bobbie squirmed at Jerry's oblique reference to his homosexuality.

"You're okay," she said finally.

"At long last I have come to believe that too," he said. "Well, back to you. In my opinion it's a good possibility that Coleman is willing to have the mayor suffer a temporary setback in public opinion in order to knock some 'sense' into his head."

"Hmm," Bobbie murmured noncommittally. "What's in the rest of these articles?"

"Read them." He handed Bobbie a slim packet of articles, clipped mainly from business sections of various newspapers.

"C.J. doesn't seem the kind of person I'd trust with my house key," she said as she put the clippings down. "Not what I'd call a nice guy."

"He'd sell his own grandmother for a buck," Jerry agreed. "It's interesting how easy it is to read between the lines. Nobody actually calls him a lying, manipulative schemer in any of these articles, but that's definitely the picture that emerges after you read a couple of them. He's done in more than one partner with his get-rich schemes, and I daresay, he's swindled a lot of unsuspecting people out of their hard-earned savings, building houses made of papier-mâché. Did you notice that there's nothing actually illegal in what he has done?"

Bobbie nodded. "It's not illegal but it is unsavory. I simply don't understand how Dan could associate with him. He can't possibly know his background."

"You said the same thing about Coleman. Our mayor is pretty smart. I think he knows whom he's dealing with and I think he knows what he's doing. But somebody here is pulling a fast one."

"What do you think?" Bobbie asked. "Is it Coleman or C.J.? And why would it be C.J.? He's the one who needs Dan to do him a favor. He wouldn't intentionally cut his own throat."

"Who understands the workings of minds like his? The devil, too, has his reasons."

"Does it make me look awfully stupid to say that I thought C.J. was sweet when I met him?" She shook her head in disgust and looked up at the ceiling. "Will somebody please take me to a Doris Day film?"

"Sorry. Even Doris Day doesn't see Doris Day films anymore."

"And what's in this last packet? Am I about to find out that Sandra is a KGB agent?" she sighed.

"Far from it." Jerry grinned.

Bobbie read the few clippings on Sandra carefully and as she did her frown deepened considerably.

"This is worse," she groaned. "High school valedictorian, college prom queen, moot-court winner in law school, third runner-up in the Miss Wisconsin contest, *and* she has a rich father! Some people have everything!"

"Not everything," Jerry retorted. "I saved the best for last." He pulled a clipping from a white envelope in his back pocket. "A typical piece of Hermani's work," he said as he handed it over.

" 'Heartbreak Hotel by any other name is called City Hall,' " she read aloud. "What's this?" She looked up.

"Read on," Jerry commanded.

" 'Sandra Wilkes, Mayor Allen's beautiful dark-haired attorney, is said to be grieving over her lost love. When questioned, she answered that the mayor can belong to no woman. He belongs to the city.' " Bobbie's laughter exploded through the room. "What garbage! Sandra would no sooner say something like that than I would. Hermani has some imagination. It's a wonder she hasn't been sued yet."

"True, but she doesn't completely invent her stories. I'm sure he did have an affair with Sandra."

"They were probably discussing law when Hermani saw them," Bobbie said quickly, feeling oddly protective of Dan's reputation, though as she remembered the intimate tone of voice Dan used on the phone with Sandra when she was at his house and the roses Sandra had received from Dan and then sent on to Bobbie, she knew it was true. "Even if they did go out, why would Sandra plant that story about Dan and C.J.? She'd have nothing to gain."

"How about revenge? Nobody likes to get dumped, and people like Sandra, who have had everything life's got to offer handed to them, especially dislike it. They have no experience with rejection, you see, so they take it especially hard. I have a feeling she's a little jealous of you. Jealousy is even more powerful an emotion than revenge, but when you mix the two together, watch out—you've got a powder keg. It's not hard to figure that you'd be blamed for the article appearing."

"That's laughable! It all sounds very pat, but I can

assure you it is pure fiction. You know, Jerry, you missed your calling. You should have been a mystery writer."

"Why are you so sure?"

"Because there's no way in the world that Sandra could consider me serious competition—not so serious that she would jeopardize her career. This is plain Bobbie Schaeffer you're talking to." She stuck out her tongue to emphasize the point.

"You may not be beauty contest material," Jerry admitted grudgingly, "but you've got something that few women have: an innocent sexuality that makes a man feel like swinging from the trees."

"Nonsense! You don't know what you're talking about." Bobbie laughed.

"I'm still a man," Jerry said in a hurt tone.

"Of course you are! I didn't mean it like that." Bobbie was immediately contrite. "It's just that this is a crazy situation. Yesterday I thought nobody had a reason to plant that story and now it looks as if everybody did. That is, if you suspend disbelief, and if you consider my role in this as a lot more important than it really is."

"Your problem," Jerry said slowly, "is an inferiority complex. Didn't you get enough love as a kid?"

"Jerry, that's enough!" Stung by his words, Bobbie paled. How could Jerry have guessed that she had, in fact, always played second fiddle to her older sister?

"Hey, I didn't want to step on any toes!"

"That's all right." Jerry was insightful or she was an open book, Bobbie thought ruefully. He never failed to guess what was on her mind, and they hadn't even known each other for very long. It was odd how sometimes you got closer to friends in a month than you had to your family in a lifetime.

"I have an idea," Jerry announced. "Why don't you go

to Nesbitt and ask him where he got his information? He likes you."

"That doesn't mean he'll tell me."

"It's worth a try. And it could clear your name with your friend."

"Let me think about it. Maybe I'll be able to get up my courage."

"I'll see you later. The news isn't going to wait for me much longer."

"Thanks an awful lot, Jerry. I know how hard you worked to get all this information."

"Forget it. That's what friends are for." Jerry lifted his burly form out of the single chair in Bobbie's office and left with a brotherly pat on her shoulder.

Bobbie sat down in the chair. It was still warm from Jerry. She too had better get some work done or her job would be standing on the unemployment lines. Not surprisingly her mind, crowded with thoughts of Dan, Coleman, C.J., and Sandra, refused to think humorous thoughts. Impatiently Bobbie decided that she would drink a cup of coffee in the lounge while she watched the afternoon news on the portable black and white TV there. That was always good for a few laughs. Today that turned out to be a mistake, for, naturally when she least wanted to see him, the mayor appeared, looking suave and dashing as a pirate on the little screen. Angrily she turned off the set. And turned it back on. He was smiling into the camera. Damn those perfect white teeth, she thought. And those deep, penetrating eyes and that fabulous, big chest. He was saying something about water conservation, she wasn't sure what, she was too busy concentrating on his mouth to listen to his words. So intent was she on the celluloid image on the screen that she didn't even hear the door to the lounge open.

"You have good taste," Hermani cackled as she stirred

her coffee. "And so does he. Sandra Wilkes was out with him last night."

Pushing her glasses back on her nose, Bobbie stalked out of the room. She would not, she swore, legitimize that woman's words with a response. When her fury subsided and the import of Hermani's words sank in, Bobbie felt a fog of depression descend upon her that she knew would be difficult to shake. Dan and Sandra. Maybe Jerry had been right when he said they were involved in a love affair. Maybe Sandra had won him back again. Maybe she had been at war with Bobbie. There were a million maybes. There was one certainty. And that was that Bobbie had better get to work. Enough of this mooning about!

Knowing that if she really did put her mind to it, nothing could stop her from creating a good cartoon, Bobbie put her hands over her eyes and thought. Maybe a half hour passed. Maybe an hour. However long it was, an idea came to her, and as soon as she touched charcoal to paper, it worked itself out in a variety of interesting sequences. It always seemed like a miracle to Bobbie. Her mind would be a blank, and then, almost as if turning on a light switch, she would begin to produce work that made her proud.

This time she parodied herself. She showed a caricature of herself looking for an idea, pouring over pictures of floods, fires, and war, trying to find the humor in them. She thought the cartoon was slightly self-indulgent but apt, because no matter what the picture, everyone saw it according to their own view of the world. As she finished the cartoon Bobbie thought that it would certainly do and might even make a mark. Most cartoonists were too insecure to laugh at themselves. But Bobbie always brought herself into her work. That was what made it special.

Though Nesbitt had told her to get the mayor, she decided that for a while at least she would concentrate on

97

international news. For whenever she read the local sections of the paper or watched the local news, she would be met by a face she wanted to avoid. Why hadn't she fallen for someone a little more anonymous?

CHAPTER VIII

On Friday Bobbie vowed that over the weekend she would not think about any news at all and especially not about Dan Allen. She swept her hands through her hair. Perhaps she would take in a movie or two. Unlike many women, Bobbie enjoyed going to the movies alone. Movies were not a social situation and she could not see the need to have another body in the seat next to hers for a security blanket. It had been a difficult week and she was going to relax. As five o'clock rolled around, Bobbie picked up her Gucci briefcase, a gift from her sister, and her slightly worn London Fog and headed for home.

It felt good to enter her little apartment. Her canary chirped in greeting and she liked to think that her goldfish swam more excitedly at her arrival. Popping a box of frozen crepes in the oven, she laughed to think how much she resembled the TV commercial for that frozen foods line: a youngish career woman with more important things on her mind than cooking dinner, for instance the hot bath she was about to draw for herself. After quickly stripping off her clothes, she let the water run and went into the living room to choose a Pinchas Zuckerman album for the stereo. There was nothing like a hot bath and the sweet strains of Zuckerman's violin for a sensuous experience. Consciously ignoring the water shortage—she promised that for penance she would take all her old soda bottles to a recycling plant next week—she let the water run continuously so that the slight seepage down the drain was immediately replenished. The sounds of the music and the sounds of the water effectively drowned out the repeated, insistent ringing of the phone.

Finished with her bath, she threw on an old pair of jeans, quickly ate her moderately artificial-tasting dinner, and hurried out to make the seven-fifteen showing of a new Robert Redford film. The movie was provocative and absorbing and got her weekend off to exactly the kind of start she wanted. She would sleep well that night.

Bobbie rolled over, groaned, and reached out her hand to shut off the alarm. But it was not the alarm that was ringing. It was the phone. Squinting in the gray dawn, she could hardly believe that someone was calling her at 6 A.M.

"Hello," she said in a thick morning voice.

"Rise and shine, morning glory," Larry's cheerful voice boomed out of the receiver.

"Is this some kind of sick joke?" Bobbie asked sleepily.

"Not at all. Jerry and I have just decided to go canoeing and we figured that a little company from the fair sex wouldn't do us any harm. Besides, we need someone to balance the lunch basket in case we spring a leak in the boat. Whaddya say?"

"Are you an ex-New Yorker?" Bobbie asked.

"How did you know? I've been a Wisconsonite for fifteen years."

"Your accent probably only comes out before eight o'clock. Canoeing, eh? Where?"

"The Menomonee River. You'll come?"

"Why not? What do I have to lose? Except my peaceful weekend. What can I bring?"

"Egg salad sandwiches and a change of clothes. We'll pick you up in half an hour."

"Wait a minute. That hardly gives me enough time to boil the eggs and find the waxed paper. Make it forty-five."

"Righto. Later."

"Later." Bobbie dropped the phone onto the receiver and pulled the covers back over her head. It was wonderfully warm under the big feather quilt that she had had since childhood. Though she knew it should be discarded because her carpet was always covered with a network of fine white feathers, she couldn't bear to part with it. For the next ten minutes she struggled with herself and finally with a languid yawn sat up and stepped onto the fuzzy floor. She'd better get those eggs on the fire! She tugged on the same jeans she had worn last night and her old college sweat shirt. At least she wouldn't be overdressed, she thought wryly as she examined herself in the mirror. In that outfit she looked like a slightly world-weary adolescent. She didn't think the fish would mind, and Jerry and Larry wouldn't have eyes for her anyway. She was just wrapping the sandwiches and gulping down her coffee as the buzzer sounded. Bobbie packed everything in a tote bag and clomped downstairs in her sturdy oxfords, once more failing to hear her phone ringing.

"Hi, guys!" She smiled as she climbed into the backseat, piled high with blankets, food, and paddles. The Volkswagen looked as if it were about to buckle under the weight of the shiny canoe that was tied onto its roof.

"Would you rather take my car?" Bobbie offered.

"This little Bug is tried and true, undaunting and loyal."

"Don't listen to him," Larry said. "He has stock in the company."

"I could have killed you when I answered the phone this morning, but I'm glad you got me out this early. We must

101

be the only three people up and around before seven on a Saturday," Bobbie noted, looking at the passing scenery. "What made you think of canoeing anyway? It's a little early in the season for it."

Larry let his hand droop mockingly. "We got tired of antiquing and of haunting the art galleries. Jerry thought he'd like to try something a little more macho today," he said in an exaggerated lisp.

"This guy's looking for a kick you know where," Jerry kidded. "I for one am fed up with winter and decided to hurry up summer. As long as we don't hit any ice floes we'll be fine, and I doubt that, since it's supposed to be in the sixties today. You did bring a jacket, didn't you?"

Bobbie showed him a parka, which she had rolled up in her tote bag along with the sandwiches. "Do you mind if I sleep till we get to the lake? I'm not much good at conversation at this hour."

"Be my guest. Put your head on the blanket and stretch out as best you can," Jerry advised.

Bobbie took him up on the offer. One of her most trea-sured talents was her ability to sleep in the oddest posi-tions and the unlikeliest places. Today was no exception, for a scant hour later she felt a hand shaking her awake.

"At least you don't snore," Jerry was saying.

"But don't tell her what she said," Larry teased. "Why, I was so embarrassed listening to you, I had to put my hands over my ears. And to think, this mayor is our respected and revered leader!" Bobbie felt herself turn purple to the roots of her hair. Taking pity on her, Jerry exploded, "Don't listen to him. He's got a strange sense of humor!"

"I was kidding," Larry admitted. "But your reaction tells me more than I want to know. And you seemed so virginal!" He was laughing. Bobbie threw a paper cup at

102

him. "You better watch and make sure I don't drown you! The river looks nice and empty."

"Can you carry the food and life jackets?" Jerry asked Bobbie.

"Sure. Two life jackets coming up!"

"She's cute, isn't she?" Larry made as if to pinch her.

Bobbie flashed him a fetching smile and bowed. "Thank you, thank you. Hey, you guys aren't intending to do all the paddling, are you? I mean we are taking turns?"

"Of course we are," Larry replied. "I wouldn't want my muscles to get too big."

"Enough already!" Jerry shouted. "It's the same joke all the time. The first time it's funny, even the second time. But when you reach two hundred, it gets a little tiring. *Capisci?*"

"He's too sensitive," Larry said in a stage whisper to Bobbie.

"The word is 'mature,' " Jerry corrected.

Bobbie laughed. She wasn't quite sure how to react to these "in" jokes about their homosexuality. She thought her best bet was to remain noncommittal. She knew that she could say something insulting, for example, about her sister, but if anyone else did she would be hurt and angry. And though Jerry and Larry seemed well adjusted, she knew that with the world the way it was, being different wasn't easy.

The men pushed the boat out into the water, where it bobbed gently up and down. Taking a big step right in the mud, Bobbie hopped into the canoe and seated herself in the middle plank.

"Don't tip us over," she warned her friends. "I just washed my hair."

"Your hair is the last thing you'd worry about if we tipped over," Jerry answered. "This river is full of underground weeds. It makes it bloody dangerous for swimming. You'd get tangled up in them and eventually pulled down."

"And the weeds would make it impossible for the police to drag the river in order to recover your body," Larry added gleefully.

"Stop being so morbid!" Bobbie said sharply.

"You get your kicks where you find them," Larry giggled.

With a look of consternation Bobbie pulled on her life jacket and warned the others to do likewise.

"Look, you've really frightened her," Larry said.

"Don't worry," Jerry said reassuringly. "I was on the canoe team at school. But I don't want to see anyone standing up or shifting suddenly. Ready?"

"Ready!" Bobbie and Larry said in unison as Jerry pushed off with his paddle. Her fears were quickly forgotten as the canoe glided over the mirror-smooth river. There was hardly a ripple in the water nor a breeze in the cool air.

"I don't suppose we'll be shooting any rapids?" Bobbie asked.

"Not quite. This is going to be a nice, tranquil day," Jerry answered. "I need tranquillity after a week at the paper, don't you?"

"You better believe it. My nerves are jangled, my head is spinning, and for the first time since I started this job, I said to myself yesterday, T.G.I.F."

"I'd like to have one of those houses over there facing the river," Larry said. "What do you say we buy one, Jerry?"

"I don't think we'd fit in right here in the northwestern suburbs of Milwaukee. This isn't San Francisco, in case you've forgotten."

"Well, then maybe we should move to San Francisco," Larry suggested.

"Hey! I don't want you guys moving. Who would befriend me—Hermani?"

"Larry's just talking. He does that periodically. He wouldn't give up his job or his city any sooner than I would."

"Good." Bobbie closed her eyes and let the motion of the canoe gently rock her to and fro. Jerry and Larry lapsed into silence and the only sounds were the chirping of birds in the trees that bordered the river and the hissing of the canoe as it slid over the thick, waterlogged undergrowth. The tranquillity nudged the turmoil that had been Bobbie's steady companion since she had first laid eyes on Dan Allen into a state of quiescence.

"Anything new with His Honor?" Larry broke the spell.

"You've got great timing," Bobbie answered wearily. "I was just forgetting about him. It's over with us, that's all."

"Are you going to talk to Nesbitt?" Jerry asked soberly.

"What about?" Larry broke in.

"Nothing that concerns you, buddy," Jerry retorted.

"I guess I'll talk to him. I've been avoiding the issue. And I'd like to continue to do so until Monday morning, okay?"

Her two friends nodded sympathetically. Larry sighed, "The perils of heterosexuality. The straight world is all messed up!"

"You're a nut!" Bobbie laughed. She closed her eyes once more, but the spell was broken. The river was no longer a solace; it became a barrier. If she were home, there was always a chance that she would run into him or even see him on television. Here she felt isolated and alone. Her friends were nice but they didn't provide the comfort, mixed though it had been with doubt, that Dan had given her. The river below was murky, uninteresting. It had been in Dan's eyes that she had felt she could drown in the limpid, deep pools that he used to see into the very depths of her soul. They could never, she feared now, cross the river of suspicion and sarcasm. They would never meet again as two people falling in love. She was the adversary. He was unattainable. And as Bobbie accepted that as truth, the day became gray for her. The steady stream of banter at which Jerry and Larry excelled began to bore her. She wanted to get home. But she had six hours to wait.

Having gone through the motions of having fun, of enjoying the picnic lunch on the grassy bank of the river, though the sulfa smell of the hard-boiled eggs nauseated her, of laughing at the jokes, of contributing to the spirit of camaraderie, Bobbie thought she deserved an Oscar. She wondered why, when it came down to brass tacks, that friendships dwindled so in importance. It was impossible to concentrate on Jerry's words or Larry's insinuations, well-meant though they were, when all she wanted to think about was Dan's sinewy arms or his sculpted lips. Bobbie felt bad, for she truly liked her friends and wanted to be with them more than in mere physical presence. She decided finally, in a fit of depression, that she was selfish and had a bad character because she could find no space in her head for anyone other than "The One," as she sometimes referred to Dan in her imagination.

The way back to the car, upriver against the current, was a long haul. Bobbie had to laugh at the feigned reluctance with which Larry abdicated to her his position at the stern of the boat. Though it was hard at first, it felt good to paddle. Those particular muscles had been in disuse for too long; she knew that tomorrow she would regret the fervor with which she attacked the water.

"I'll probably be too stiff to walk tomorrow," she complained lightly.

"You'll be in traction," Jerry assured her.

"I'll bring you over some chicken soup," Larry offered.

"Does that work for charley horses too?"

"Chicken soup works for whatever ails you," Larry said with absolute certainty.

"And all along everybody thought that penicillin was the miracle drug," Bobbie parried.

"It just goes to show how much the medical establishment knows," Larry stated. With a yawn he leaned back and stretched out his arms above his head. "Man, this is the life: sunning myself while you two paddle yourselves to the point of exhaustion. It must be nice to have a slave. You wanna be my slave, Bobbie?"

"Sorry, my calendar's booked for the next hundred years."

"Bobbie's already a slave—to her heart," Jerry joined in.

"Boo! That was bad. Any tomatoes left? This one deserves a couple of soft ones in the face," Larry said, diverting attention from Bobbie's pained expression. Bobbie didn't reply, preferring to concentrate on the steady rhythm of her dipping and pulling.

"Does your arm still hurt?" Jerry asked after a while.

"No, I don't even know I have an arm anymore. It's completely numb."

"You want me to take your place?" Larry offered.

"Isn't he the generous one? We're a hundred yards from the pier," Jerry said wryly.

"That's all right," Bobbie answered. "Pain builds character, so they say." Her brave front to the contrary, the last stretch seemed like a hundred miles and left Bobbie convinced that she was a city mouse and you couldn't put a city mouse in the country.

If Bobbie was a poor conversationalist on the way out that morning, it was nothing compared to the way home. So cramped was she after sitting for an entire day in one position that she hobbled to the car and could barely manage a groan as she collapsed in the backseat.

"This scratchy, torn, cluttered seat feels like a Rolls-Royce to me now" was all she said before she lapsed into total silence.

"We've got a frontierswoman with us," Larry gibed. Even Jerry was too tired to respond.

"Thanks for asking me to come," Bobbie said as they pulled up to her apartment. "It was fun."

"Yeah, it was great," Jerry agreed with the same lack of conviction.

"Maybe next week we can all get together and go to a wine-tasting party," Larry said. "I think that's more our speed."

"Bye, guys. And thanks again. I mean it!" Bobbie waved them off cheerfully. She did mean it. They *were* nice guys.

CHAPTER IX

The best thing about exhaustion and sweat was coming home to a hot shower. The water, as it pounded into the sore muscles of her back, was therapeutic. And she had to admit to herself that there was something deliciously healthy about the physical exhaustion that she suffered. It was certainly to be preferred over the mental stress that had assailed her these last few days. Stepping out of the shower, she wrapped her wet hair turban style in a large yellow turkish towel and snuggled into a soft terry-cloth robe of the same color. She curled up on her living room sofa with a cup of hot herbal tea and a pile of magazines that begged to be read. And then there was a knock on her door. Her heart pounded, for she wasn't expecting anyone and seldom received unannounced visitors. Crime, unfortunately, was on everyone's mind these days.

"Who's there?" she asked tremulously as she stood on tiptoe to look through the peephole. She thought she was seeing things. It was Dan. She opened the door but stood there blocking his entrance and staring at him silently.

"May I come in?" he said finally.

Bobbie moved aside, self-conscious in her bathrobe, towel, and totally unadorned face. She was feeling at a decided disadvantage as she faced an impeccably dressed and groomed mayor.

"I don't think this is quite the moment for me to entertain," she muttered.

"I don't want to be entertained. I want to talk to you," he growled. "Where have you been all day? I've been calling every half hour."

"Canoeing," she answered shortly.

"Canoeing! And I suppose tomorrow you'll be off bear trapping? I never would have thought you were the outdoors type."

"What did you think? That I was the bedroom type?" she asked acidly.

"No, but now that you mention it . . ." He grinned, as his eyes flickered over her body. Bobbie drew the belt of her robe tighter around her.

"If you're here to stay, I'd better get dressed. Excuse me." He grabbed her shoulder as she turned to go.

"Don't bother. You look very fetching. I like natural women."

"Natural is a kind way of putting it," Bobbie said, laughing defensively.

"No, it's not. Most of the women I come in contact with wear so much makeup, I wouldn't know them without it if I fell over them. A man goes to bed with a woman like that and he could be in for a bad shock when the lights go on."

"I don't know why you're talking about bed."

Dan laughed. "All right, shall we discuss stock options?"

"That sounds interesting," Bobbie said coolly. "But I think I would like to postpone this conversation to a later date. I'm tired."

"Had a hard day, eh? Who accompanied you on this boating trip—or shouldn't I ask?"

"You have no reason to know but I'll tell you anyway just to be polite. I went with Jerry and Larry."

110

"They're safe enough."

"What's that supposed to mean?"

"Just that I don't have to fear the competition."

"I didn't know there was a competition," she answered waspishly. "And I didn't know I was the prize."

"You are a prize," he said caressingly as he moved closer to her. "And I'm going to win you."

"And after you've won me," she spat out, "what do you do, go on to the next competition and the next and the next . . . ?"

Moving yet closer to her, he said in a menacing tone of voice, "You've got something of the shrew in you, and I have something of the tamer in me. Come here." He pulled her to him and kissed her roughly. Bobbie struggled against him, her lips sealed and her palms pushing against his chest with all her might. Rather than securing her release, her efforts succeeded only in tightening his viselike grip.

"Don't fight me, baby," he whispered hoarsely in her ear as he kissed its delicate lobe.

Bobbie found herself on the verge of tears. It wasn't because she was unhappy in her predicament but rather because she was filled with an emotion she was afraid to express. His strength astonished her. Yes, he was a big man and she knew he was strong, but his hands, she thought now, felt like fire and his will was of iron. She would not be able to keep up this charade forever. He would know soon how much she wanted him, how thoughts of him crowded everything else out of her head, and then he would leave her and go on to the next conquest. Reputations weren't simply invented. They might, she knew as a media person, be exaggerated, but they were almost always based on the truth. Dan Allen was known as a lady killer, a heartbreaker, a Don Juan. There were a million epithets for a man like Dan Allen and none of them was flattering, not unless you were a masochist, which Bobbie was not. And Bobbie was sure, as sure as she could be of anything, that she was not the woman, if indeed one existed, to change him. For she was relatively inexperienced in the world of love, and when feminine wiles were passed out, she was not even on line. How could she fight him? Hadn't he known he had won her when he first smiled into her eyes? It had been a long time since Bobbie had felt desire for a man, but now she could barely keep herself from begging him to take her. But she had to stay in control. She had to.

He covered her face with his kisses and reached up to free her hair from the towel. As the damp strands fell onto her shoulders he bent to kiss her neck, still holding her tight. The rough skin of his face made her skin glow pink against her yellow bathrobe. With one hand he untied the robe and purposefully and slowly caressed her breast. If she had any thought to resist, Bobbie knew it was hopeless. She clung to him now, and as she threw her face back to meet his mouth with hers, a whimper escaped her lips.

"Do you want me?" he asked, though he couldn't help but know the answer. Bobbie understood that he wanted to hear it from her, his victory. It embarrassed her to admit it but there was no help for her.

"Yes, I want you, I want you. You can't know how much."

"Do you like when I do this to you?" He bent to kiss her breasts.

"Oh, Dan, yes. I like it." Her voice broke. In a flash she felt herself lifted up in his arms. The belt to her bathrobe lay useless on the floor and with the terry cloth trailing behind her she was, as before, naked under his gaze.

"This way to the bedroom?" He indicated the closed door with his head.

"Yes," Bobbie replied as she buried her face in his neck.

112

It felt strange to be carried like that. It was terribly gothic, she ruminated with the one rational part of her mind. He laid her down gently on the bed with its bright flowered sheets. Looking up at him she saw fire in his eyes as he towered above her.

"Now, my pretty, will you make a cartoon out of this scene?"

"Is that why you've got me here like this?" she faltered. "To mock me?"

"No, the reasons, I think, are rather more apparent," he countered. An urgent message to cover her nakedness reached her brain and she pulled her robe across her and held it closed with folded arms.

"Not an instant replay of last time," he scoffed.

"It won't happen again," she said crisply. "I've been a fool."

"You're being a fool now. Don't spoil it, Bobbie. You're overly sensitive and you can't take a joke. Back up."

"So it's attack Bobbie's character time, is it? I'm sorry you don't approve of me, but there are plenty of thick-skinned ladies out there who I am sure will be happy to service you."

Dan managed a strained smile. "Three strikes and you're out, baby. You've got one left."

"Don't do me any favors. I withdraw."

With his back to her, Dan moved stiffly to the window. Though the thunderclouds hid his face from view, she could see a muscle tick at the back of his cheek. Momentarily ashamed of herself, Bobbie put her hands over her face. Why did she always act like a frightened schoolgirl, like a tease? She was twenty-seven years old and had already had one long love affair. It wasn't as if this were the Middle Ages and she had to protect her maidenhood. Why was she constantly putting an obstacle in the way of their lovemaking? Dan was right; she *was* too sensitive.

113

But he couldn't know the reason. Never before in her life had Bobbie been out of control. She had always judged others well and had measured out her own feelings. Since her teens she had known that she wanted to control her destiny, to be master of her fate. She had scorned her classmates who lived for their Saturday-night dates, for she had known that there was much more to life than the masquerade called romance. But with Dan all that had changed. As a tidal wave destroys all in its path so Dan swept away her reserve and her will. It was true that she didn't believe he was deeply interested in her, for Bobbie knew what she was: attractive, bright, a nice person. But she wasn't beautiful or glamorous. She didn't have the *Playboy* look that Dan's women possessed. This was a mere dalliance for him. It was, she confessed to herself, the only thrilling interlude in her life. And she didn't want it to ruin her life. She didn't want to lose her self-esteem or her direction. Once he made love to her, there would be no turning back. Bobbie Schaeffer, the up-and-coming cartoonist, would be just one more seduced and abandoned career woman.

As she removed her hands from her eyes she looked up to see Dan gazing at her with a thoughtful expression.

"I don't want to fight with you," he said. "Get dressed. I'll wait in the other room." He closed the door behind him.

As Bobbie rose obediently and walked marionettelike to her closet, she heard him pacing back and forth in the living room. She picked out a Sasson jean skirt and a blue and white pin-striped shirt. There was nothing sexy about the outfit but she was satisfied that it was "her." She ran a brush through her uncombed hair. Drying without the benefit of a blower, it was a mass of tangles. There was nothing to be done but to sweep it severely back from her face and pin it up. Maybe her inner beauty would shine

114

through, she thought wryly. Well, it didn't matter anyway. As she entered the living room Dan whirled around to face her. His mouth was unremittingly hard.

"Sit down. I want you to listen to what I have to say." Bobbie sat on the edge of her repro Queen Anne.

"You think I'm some kind of monster, some kind of salacious lecher who's waiting for the opportunity to have sex with you and then live to laugh about it. I can assure you," he said sarcastically, "your friends on the paper would see me dead and buried symbolically, if not physically, before that could happen. And, if I can be so crude, I've had women before you—"

"And you'll have women after me," she cut in.

"Don't put words in my mouth," he snapped in exasperation. "You're one of the few people who make me lose my temper—you and my mother."

"I'm not sure how I should take that."

"Don't analyze everything. That's your trouble. You don't take things at face value."

"You, for instance?"

"Yes, me! And let me finish. I've had sexier women than you—"

"That's not news. And you don't have to finish, I've heard it before." Bobbie turned slightly so he couldn't see the tears glistening in her eyes. But Dan ignored her and continued louder than before.

"I've had sexier women than you but none lovelier." Bobbie turned to look at him.

"Yes, I mean it," he reiterated. "You're lovely, you have wit and brains, and I feel good when I'm at your side—despite the fact that you seem to enjoy beating me down. I don't enjoy that too much, but I think I understand why you do it. You've seen my name linked with"— he laughed sardonically—"the beauties of our time. They are so boring. Yes, I was with them but I was lonely with

115

them. I'm not lonely with you. You're grounded and I know you're there and I know you understand what I say and that you can respond to me in every way. Do I have to go on?" She shook her head. A smile lit up her eyes.

"That's good," he stated, "because this sort of tribute isn't my style. So I hope you won't expect a daily dose of flattery. This may be the last time you'll get any. Do I make myself understood?"

"Oh, Dan. I don't know what to say."

"Are you happy?" he asked huskily.

"Yes, I'm happy. I'm very happy." She walked over to him and, standing on her tiptoes, planted a light kiss on his cheek.

"Enough of that for one day," he said brusquely, pushing her away. "Let's go out and get something to eat."

"Whatever you say." She smiled shyly. "I'll get my coat." She paused then and with a note of trepidation creeping into her voice she said, "There is one thing, Dan."

"What's that, honey?" Goose bumps arose on her arms as she heard the unfamiliar endearment.

"Do you still think I planted that story about you and C.J.?"

"I don't think about it," he answered shortly.

"Dan!" Bobbie felt panic engulf her. It had been too good to be true!

"I don't think you'd do something like that, at least not intentionally," he conceded. "Maybe you were talking to a friend who didn't turn out to be trustworthy or maybe someone else overheard. There are all sorts of possible explanations. You're naive when it comes to that dog-eat-dog world out there, even if you do have an impressive job. All you have to do is tell one person and that's it."

"I swear to you, Dan. Not a word of that story was my

fault. I don't know who leaked it, but it wasn't me. I'm not as naive as you think," she added lamely.

"There's no sense discussing it. We won't find any answers. Chinese or Indian?"

"Huh?"

"Do you want to eat at a Chinese restaurant or an Indian one?"

"A very hot chicken curry would hit the spot," she said brightly, though she was feeling a bit subdued. While there was a shadow of doubt in Dan's mind, things could not be perfect. And with Dan Allen she could not settle for less than perfection.

The restaurant to which Dan escorted her was called Shiva. It was Milwaukee's newest Indian restaurant and quite popular since the rave reviews it had received from the food critics of the city's two major newspapers. Although there was a line of about ten people waiting, Dan was recognized immediately and given a choice corner table.

"That's a good way to build up resentment among your constituents," Bobbie noted.

"Not at all. I tipped my hat to them. And they can tell their friends they dine at the same place as the mayor. It's an even trade."

"You don't wear a hat!" Bobbie laughed. "And I may have mentioned before that your cynicism gives me the shivers."

"I do my job well and that's all that matters. Though with the pressures of this office building up and the reelection campaign soon to be launched, I must say I could do with a vacation."

"Maybe in the next decade," she teased.

"Why don't we skip dinner and catch the next flight to Bermuda?" Bobbie caught the jesting yet wistful note in his voice.

"Bermuda? How prosaic. I'll settle for nothing less than a trek up the Himalayas in search of the Abominable Snowman."

"Sounds great. But I wouldn't know how much to tip the Sherpa guides."

"Okay, you convinced me." Bobbie laughed. "Let's go to the zoo on your next free day."

He looked up from his menu. "I'm having the Tandoori Chicken. How about you?"

"I made up my mind an hour ago. It's the chicken curry."

"Next time I cook dinner for you I'll make a curry. It's easy enough, if you buy a good brand of curry powder," Dan offered gallantly.

Bobbie laughed. "Dan, the spaghetti dinner you made after the baseball game was superb. You do a mean job of opening a jar of spaghetti sauce and I know you could do as well with curry powder. But now I'm going to educate you. In India there is no such thing as curry powder. Curry is a mixture of all kinds of spices, turmeric and garlic among others. Curry powder is to Indian cuisine as frozen egg rolls are to Chinese cuisine."

Dan clutched his hands to his heart. "Stop! You've mortally wounded me."

"Now who's being sensitive?" Bobbie smiled. "Anyway, the truth of the matter is that you could toast me a piece of white bread and it would taste better than the flakiest croissant out of the finest French bakery."

"Talking about flaky!"

"Do you know," Bobbie said, "that since I've met you I've been eating out more than I have in the past two years? This high living may spoil me forever."

"I think you're unspoilable."

"Flattery will get you everywhere." Bobbie laughed.

"But," Dan continued, "since I don't take unnecessary

chances, perhaps I'd better put you to work. I have a lot of papers that I have to take care of tomorrow and a lot of envelopes that need stuffing. How about if you come over to my office in the morning and we can have Sunday brunch from the electric pan and then rub elbows over some work. It will be our last chance to see each other for a week. I have to leave tomorrow night for Washington. I'm going to rustle up some funds for our fair city."

"You're forgetting, dear heart, that my political beliefs are as far from yours as they can get. Even if I were your mother, I couldn't vote for you, so how could I work in your campaign?"

"I don't think our values are that far apart," Dan said reproachfully. "It's our tactics that are different. We both believe that our country should have a sound economy and that people are America's most valuable resource. It's just that you believe in giving the poor their food whereas I believe in teaching them how to grow it."

"Don't throw your campaign slogan out at me. It's simplistic rubbish," Bobbie said crisply. "But fodder for a very good cartoon!" Her eyes twinkled mischievously.

"Are you going to make me regret that statement?"

"You'll find out when you read the afternoon edition of the *Post.* All's fair in love, war, and politics! But since you gave me inspiration for Monday's work, I think I can, in good conscience, stuff some envelopes for you. The damage my cartoon will do you will more than balance any help I give by stuffing envelopes!"

"My feet are quaking in my shoes," Dan said laughingly. "But I can't have my woman laughing at me in public or you'll find that soon no one will take neither you nor me seriously."

"My private life has little to do with my career," Bobbie retorted with a spark in her eyes. "And I'm certain it's the same for you."

119

Dan studied her with a faintly amused scowl. "Defiance makes your eyes light up. The puzzle is how to rid you of your defiance yet maintain the light. Shall I beat it out of you? Take you over my knee, pull down your panties, and spank that round bottom till it glows a bright pink and till you beg me to stop and promise your obedience?"

Bobbie squirmed. "You wouldn't dare!"

"Do you care to put me to the test?" Dan asked smoothly.

"The food's here," Bobbie said in evident relief as the waiter set the spicy dishes before them.

The rest of the meal was passed in light chatter and proved altogether uneventful. Whether he talked philosophy or small talk, politics or weather talk, Dan was glib and absorbing. At home in bed that night Bobbie was amazed at how interested she had been in soy beans, municipal bonds, and cloud formations. She supposed that was what was meant when people said that Dan Allen possessed charisma.

CHAPTER X

Bobbie was at City Hall bright and early the following Sunday morning. It was a pleasure driving downtown: the traffic was sparse and the only people out that early were churchgoers and a few joggers along the lake. And to think, Bobbie mused, she had looked forward to a quiet weekend with nothing more exciting than the movies. This was infinitely better, if more fatiguing. She wondered what mayors did when they were married and had families. Did the wives and children stuff envelopes on weekends or did they stumble along as best they could without a man around the house? She *was* jumping the gun! Bobbie thought. Here she had had one date with him that didn't end in an argument and she was already practically naming the kids! As she entered the impressive building that housed the mayor's offices, Bobbie was approached by a security guard who asked for her identification. She signed her name with a flourish in the visitors' book and with anticipation rode the elevator to the top floor and the hubbub of decision-making. She had expected to be working alone with Dan but now she saw with a start that there were messengers running back and forth looking self-important, aides and volunteers, and—for all the rotten luck —there was Coleman glaring at her. Hesitantly Bobbie took a step backward, for her impulse was to escape, but then she heard Dan calling to her.

121

"Good morning," he boomed. "Come over here. Coleman, get the lady a cup of coffee."

Though she dragged her feet a little, Bobbie walked over to Dan with a casual gait. She smiled wanly in greeting. "I hope Coleman won't put arsenic in my coffee," she whispered.

"I told you not to worry about him," Dan whispered back. "He's only half human. The other half is pure robot."

"I'll stay," she said doubtfully, "as long as you're sure you've got him programmed right."

Dan grinned as Coleman came back with Bobbie's coffee. "Loosen up, Coleman. You're spooking my friend." Coleman mumbled a reply that Bobbie didn't hear and turned his back to her as he headed for his desk.

"I don't choose my aides for their personalities," Dan said in apology. "He's effective in his job and in some twisted way he thinks he's protecting me. I suppose he doesn't realize that I'm king of the beasts."

"Show me how you're king," Bobbie taunted.

"I refuse to address that remark in public," Dan answered laconically. "Let me introduce you to Mrs. Hallman, who will show you what to do."

Mrs. Hallman was a plump, motherly lady who soon had Bobbie comfortably working behind a long wooden table piled with papers and envelopes. Bobbie didn't even read the material she was putting into the envelopes; she knew she wouldn't agree with it and she didn't want to aggravate herself. She rationalized that she wasn't really helping the opposition in any crucial way, for the envelopes would get stuffed with or without her and at least she was near Dan and could, whenever she caught his eye, let herself feel deliciously sinful.

Thus the morning stretched into afternoon. Dan had been too busy to pay her more than scant attention, so

Bobbie had little to show for her efforts other than a few paper cuts on her fingers. When with the striking of three o'clock Sandra breezed in wearing an inappropriately low-cut black sweater over slinky silk pants, the entire office seemed to hold its collective breath. Bobbie saw Dan's eyes flicker over Sandra unceremoniously, and felt a stab of pain in her gut that almost made her cry out. Without greeting anyone else, Sandra headed straight for Dan and bent over his desk as she spoke to him in hushed tones. The only view Bobbie had now was of her tight derriere, though she imagined all too vividly the exposed cleavage under Dan's nose. It appeared to Bobbie, as she seethed with anger, that Dan was not averse to the spectacle, for she noticed that his eyes were not directed upward. She wondered how many dozens of yellow roses that view was worth. Dan's laughter suddenly pierced the quiet room and then came the musical notes of Sandra's answering laugh. Shifting her weight suggestively, Sandra continued talking to Dan, who, Bobbie noted with disgust, was paying rapt attention.

Aware of her own dowdy appearance in a Kilgarry kilt and blue blouse, Bobbie decided that she was not going to take any more of this. So she was a fool, but fifty other people did not have to bear witness to that fact. She wasn't quite sure in her confusion what Dan's game was and what perverse pleasure he got from it, but she did know that whatever it was she wasn't going to be the pawn. Bidding a hasty good-bye to Mrs. Hallman, who looked at her with what Bobbie interpreted as pity, she stumbled out to the elevator, whose closing doors she just cleared. Visions of that gorgeous black-haired lawyer crowded her mind and plunged her into the darkest of moods. Why was Mayor Dan Allen doing this to her? Was it that her cartoons had angered him so, that he planned to get revenge in the best possible way—by breaking her heart and letting the whole city laugh about it? That could be it. It could be that he had no sense of humor at all and that he had been stung by her caricatures. If so, he had played his hand with unmatched expertise. He had been right when he said she was naive. But he hadn't played fair. He should have picked someone his own size. She was strictly Little League. As she ran to her car Bobbie determined that this was the end. His game had been played out and gone into overtime. Neither apologies nor vapid explanations would move her.

"Of course," she said aloud, "he has no need to ever approach me again. His point has been well made, and everybody who works for him will know how little they have to fear from the deflated opposition." Tears flooded her eyes. Though she hated him then and felt thoroughly abused, feelings of hurt and disappointment dominated her sentiments. It would have been lovely, just like a fairy tale. But fairy tales are for children, she sighed miserably. Enough mooning over something that never was! she warned herself. Enough! There was no sense in making a bad situation worse. At least he was leaving tonight for a week so she wouldn't have to see the triumphant smirk on his face if she ran into him again. That would give her enough time to get her life in order and to salvage what little was left of her pride. Coleman would be happy when he found out what his boss had been up to, she thought bitterly. It had probably been he who had planted that story about the mayor and C.J.—anything to throw suspicion on Bobbie. That had been the fly in the ointment for Dan. He hadn't counted on an overzealous employee.

Somehow Bobbie couldn't face going home to an empty apartment. Stopping at a phone booth, she called her sister in Fond du Lac, who happily was home and eager to see Bobbie. There was a drugstore across the street so, leaving her parking lights blinking, Bobbie ran in to buy a toothbrush, for she had decided to spend the night at her sister's and to leave for work from there the next morning.

The reunion was a happy one. Her little niece and nephew were adorable, so much so, that she felt the stirrings of maternal feeling in her own breast. That was simply not fated to be, she believed ardently. Anyway, it was nicer to be an aunt than a mother. This way you got to play with them and cuddle them but didn't have to wake up for midnight feedings or wipe runny noses. And you didn't have to sacrifice your career or be married and have your life reduced to rolling sock balls. Still it would be nice to be called Mommy. . . .

Her sister was radiant. She looked more beautiful than ever and was content. She had heard rumors about Dan Allen and questioned Bobbie carefully. Bobbie was quick to assure her that there was nothing to tell and that in the romance department things were a big zero.

"I'm not cut in your mold," Bobbie said simply. "Marriage is not for me. I've got my job and my apartment. Don't worry. I'm happy. Really I am." Her sister nodded sagely and didn't say any more about it.

Bobbie helped put the kids to bed and read them each a story. Then she and her sister and brother-in-law spent the rest of the evening playing electronic video games, which her brother-in-law took great pleasure in winning, swapping stories, and looking at the family album.

That's the story of my life, she thought ruefully as she flipped the plastic pages of the photo album. There was Bobbie at age five, too busy cutting out colored paper to pause and smile for the camera. Her sister at age six was posing prettily with demurely crossed ankles and folded hands. At age ten there was hardly a picture of Bobbie without bandaged knees and skinned elbows, touting a pair of roller skates or attempting to hide in a tree from the probing camera lens. Her sister would be curtsying in

125

the tutu she wore to ballet class on Saturday mornings. And so it went. At age fifteen Bobbie was wearing glasses and in her pictures she was always carrying, as a foil, either a book or a sketchpad. Her sister was a cheerleader and looked and played the role to prefection. There weren't many pictures of Bobbie at age twenty or thereafter. She had learned to absent herself whenever the camera was brought out.

It was a wonder that Bobbie felt as close to her sister now as she did. For it was her sister who all through childhood and adolescence had preened in the sunlight and gleefully permitted Bobbie to live in her shadow. Bobbie had been blessed with a strong psyche. The only mark the experience had left on her, even with a mother who let it be known that she preferred sunshine girls, was a determination to be independent and successful.

As she lay in bed that night in the guest room, Bobbie forgot about her unhappy childhood. Her last thoughts were of Dan. She couldn't fault herself for having trusted him and succumbed to his charm. He had awakened needs and desires in her that she had worked hard to squelch. But his cruel joke, as his laughter rang out with Sandra's, had sounded the death knell to those same desires.

CHAPTER XI

As Bobbie bent over her drawing board she heard a shuffling behind her. There was Larry in an exaggerated pantomine of an old, bent man.

"Have you recovered from Saturday? Do you have any Ben-Gay? I forgot mine."

"Exercise is good for you." Bobbie smiled. "And cut it out. You're a vigorous, young, twenty-four-year-old man."

"Tell that to my aching bones," he complained. "Where were you yesterday? We tried to call you to find out if you wanted us to send over our masseur."

"Don't ask," Bobbie said shortly.

"Uh-oh," Larry intoned. "Say no more. The pained expression over the bridge of your nose tells volumes. Why don't you forget the mayor? He's not worth this agony. Just leave it to me. I'll fix you up with my cousin Seymour. You'll love him. And a little makeup will do wonders for those worry lines." He pointed at Bobbie's brow.

"Thanks for the offer but I'm swearing off men."

"I've tried that many times myself. It doesn't work," Larry sighed. "What are you doing there?" Larry leaned over Bobbie's shoulder to glance at the rough sketch of a cartoon. "That's sensational," he chuckled. "You've got him now. This is one cartoon Mayor Allen won't live down. And I'll wager that in the future he'll be more judicious about the women he exploits. I think I'll get you a 'Words Woman' T-shirt for your birthday. That'll teach him. I'll get back to work now myself. *Ciao.*"

"*Ciao,*" Bobbie replied mirthfully. Larry always made her laugh. "But I'm not doing this cartoon for revenge. The idea occurred to me and I thought it was apropos and—"

Larry winked as he stepped through the doorway. "Hey, no explanations are necessary! It's great! Great!"

With a critical eye Bobbie examined her work. It needed refining and polishing but the basic idea was good. One of the promises Dan had made in his campaign and which was widely associated with him was welfare reform. Instead of handing people their money each month, he wanted to teach them skills and get them jobs so they could earn their checks from the government. He claimed to be heading toward a virtual elimination of welfare. That his aim was admirable nobody denied. But the zealousness wrought by this desire for reform would leave many a helpless person by the wayside. Mothers of young children, the children themselves who had the misfortune to be born into a situation that was none of their doing, the elderly: all these people were bound to suffer if Mayor Allen's welfare bill went through. It wasn't, Bobbie believed, that Dan was heartless or cruel. It was simply that in every situation some people were victimized for what others perceived to be a greater good. Bobbie felt that in this case it was preferable for an overtaxed middle class to suffer rather than an innocent child. Her cartoon succinctly portrayed her point of view. The mayor was gnawing on a lobster claw while he addressed a classroom full of babies and old people. His slogan, "Don't give the poor their dinner; teach them to produce it," was emblazoned on a banner that hung across the front of the classroom.

128

And there was the mayor reading from a technical manual on the care and maintenance of tractors.

Nodding to herself, Bobbie tore the cartoon from her drawing pad and started her fourth draft. It needed cleaning up. As she had grown as an artist Bobbie had come to adopt as her credo that less is more. Where she could rid her work of a line, an angle, a shading, she did so. The results, in their starkness, were extraordinarily effective and to the point. It was two hours and four more drafts later until Bobbie was satisfied with her work. Stretching her cramped arms and stepping over the pile of discarded papers on the floor, she took the cartoon and headed for Nesbitt's office, secure in the knowledge that she had finished way before deadline.

"I like it," Nesbitt said in his no-nonsense voice. After rifling through a sheaf of papers on his desk, he held up Bobbie's file.

"You're working out better than I expected. You were hired to do three cartoons a week and you're turning in almost five usable ones per week. That leaves a nice cushion. We're budgeted for an assistant cartoonist and I was intending to start interviewing, but at the rate you're producing I feel the money would be better spent elsewhere." He looked up as if expecting Bobbie's comment.

Bobbie thought it odd that she had been in awe of Nesbitt all this time. Rather than the fearsome boss he had always seemed, she saw him now as a middle-aged man with a receding hairline, round stomach, and handlebar mustache to proclaim his identity. The furrows over his brow were deeply etched and the veins on his checks stood out in a red crisscross pattern. How he had ever frightened her Bobbie was at a loss to explain. She would never again see him as anything other than the harried, overworked city editor who wasn't quite comfortable talking with women and who therefore wasted no time on idle chatter.

"Thanks for your vote of confidence, but if you don't mind, I'd prefer that you hold your decision about that assistant in abeyance for a while. You never can tell when the springs of creativity will run dry. And something might always come up. I might get appendicitis, for heaven's sake."

"Or married," Nesbitt said dryly.

"That's one eventuality that will never take place."

"You're making sure of that with cartoons like this one. Your"—he cleared his throat—"romance with our mayor is no secret. I like what you've done here"—he indicated her cartoon—"but I don't get it." He scratched his head. "If I were Mr. Allen, I would drop you faster than a rattlesnake."

"Well then, it's a good thing you're not Mr. Allen. But never mind, there's nothing to this much-touted romance of ours."

"That's your business." Nesbitt cleared his throat again.

Bobbie was nonplussed, for Nesbitt had never displayed any curiosity about her private life. Indeed he had never related to her as anything other than a cartoonist. That the proper Germanic editor would pry into her affairs gave Bobbie pause. It hadn't occurred to her before, but now she thought that there was a good chance she and Dan were the hottest gossip item around. She decided to press the unexpected advantage that Nesbitt's atypical behavior afforded her.

"Mr. Nesbitt, you ran a story last week about the mayor and the owner of the Wildcats. Who was your source?"

With a sharp intake of breath Nesbitt began drumming his fingers on his desktop. "You know I can't answer that question, Bobbie. That information is privileged."

"I know that, but you see there are several people who

think it was me. It would mean an awful lot to me to clear my name."

Nesbitt looked at her sharply. "Are you corroborating the story?"

"No, of course not," Bobbie averred, taking a step backward. "And why should it be necessary? You are satisfied with the reliability of your source?"

It was Nesbitt's turn to hesitate. "I suppose so. We checked out the story as best we could. But you know how it is with hearsay. There were no papers copied, nothing like that."

"That's because there's nothing to back up those allegations. They're false. They don't show the whole picture— not by a long shot!" Bobbie blurted out. With an unuttered expletive she hit her hand to her head as she realized what she had said.

"So you do know something about it," Nesbitt said quietly. "It looks like we have a problem with conflict of interests."

"I told you what I know. Dan Allen is innocent of those charges. He didn't fix any loan papers for C. J. Forstader and he didn't make any promises. And in addition to printing a libelous story you're jeopardizing the reputation of this paper," Bobbie said heatedly. "You're supposed to check out your sources!" Unaware of what had come over her, Bobbie whitened as she heard the words she was tossing at her boss. No one talked to him that way. But she had done it and she might as well accept the consequences gracefully. "I'll have my desk cleared out by this afternoon," she said hoarsely.

"That won't be necessary," Nesbitt countered blandly. "Just get back to work and we'll discuss this no further. I will say one thing however: My source has impeccable credentials. I admire your loyalty to your friend, your ex-friend, or whatever he is, and I hope that loyalty extends to this newspaper. Unfortunately for you, my 'source' is privy to more information and in greater detail than you, and unless I'm dealing with a kook, I have no choice but to trust that information. Good day."

Taken aback at the abrupt dismissal, Bobbie skulked out of the office, her mind in a whirl. He had named no names but Nesbitt had implied that the source was somebody pretty close to the mayor. Who could it be? Coleman? She had previously dismissed him as a serious contender for the unwholesome tag of spy, but it looked as if he were the guilty party. That should teach Dan to deal with fanatical types, Bobbie mused.

On the way back to her office Bobbie stopped at the ladies' room. A fine mist of perspiration covered her face and the icy water she splashed on herself did wonders.

"I do my washing at home" came a familiar voice.

Bobbie whirled around to face Hermani, her mouth twisted derisively. With a sinking heart Bobbie thought that she wasn't up to dodging the barbs Hermani loved to fling.

"Hello, Hermani. How are you?"

"Fine and soon to be better. I was just on my way to duplicate these photos that were taken last night. Have you seen them yet?" With evident glee she took out a packet of Polaroid snapshots of Dan and Sandra waving from the top of the boarding ramp of a Northwest Orient plane.

"They're very nice. My compliments to the photographer," Bobbie said calmly. She thought she ought to win critical acclaim for her performance, for shock waves at Dan's blatant betrayal warred with fury at Hermani's blatant cattiness. Reeling from the hurt, Bobbie barely got a grip on herself. If she was going to forge a career at this paper, it wouldn't do to have enemies, especially one of Hermani's ilk. Unable to comprehend the reason for Hermani's animosity, she decided that the best tactic would be to confront it head on.

"Hermani, you've made it perfectly clear that you find me intolerable. Quite frankly, I'm not terribly taken with you either. But we're working here together and life is too short to muck it up with this trivia, so what do you say we call a truce?"

"I haven't the slightest idea what you're talking about, dahlink!" Hermani called over her shoulder as she swept out of the ladies' room, leaving Bobbie to squeeze a rolled-up paper towel in frustration. Within a matter of seconds the door was reopened and Hermani was back, her eyes glinting with malice. "Let's get one thing straight," she spat out. "This is *my* newsroom. I am the queen here. You, you're a small-time girl playing in a world where you don't belong. You can't compete with the mayor's attorney and you can't compete with me. So get out. Find yourself a job drawing ads for a magazine. Because if you don't get out, you'll be hurt even more than you already have. I've just been warming up. Do I make myself clear?"

"Perfectly. But what you don't understand is that this is a changing world. Even if I left, you wouldn't be the only female here for very long. There would soon be a bevy of young lovelies to take my job and other jobs. And I don't mean only in the steno pool. Didn't you hear of feminism, Hermani? Women are supposed to help each other, not step on each other."

"Don't lecture me, dear." Hermani's jaw fell though she spat out the words. "The only thing you could teach me is how to laugh with a girlish giggle, and I prefer not to learn that. It's simply nauseating. You ought to hear yourself." Hermani looked at herself in the mirror, fluffed her tightly curled hair, and tightened the narrow belt of her tailored linen suit.

"Why do you hate me, Hermani?"

"I don't hate anyone. I hate what you represent. The cartoonist you replaced, you may have heard, moved to *The Washington Post*. He had a mind that ranked with Herblock and Jules Feiffer—simply brilliant. How he made me laugh! Wherever I look I see the slipping of standards in the name of equality. A young girl like you shouldn't be in this position. You haven't earned it and you're not equal to the task."

"There are many people who wouldn't agree with your assessment of my work," Bobbie answered in a tight, controlled voice.

"They don't see past your ingenuous smile," Hermani harrumphed.

"Perhaps if you teach me to cackle, my work will be judged on its merit," Bobbie retorted.

"So you've learned the art of insult, have you? You know how to banter. That's a good start."

"I didn't know I was bantering, but if you say so . . ." Bobbie said flippantly. "Brilliant minds, you know, aren't simply born. They're nurtured and developed. My cartoons aren't all that bad for the creation of a twenty-seven-year-old brain." Bobbie's pride had been stung, and though she knew she shouldn't be defending herself, she couldn't help it.

"It's bad form to pat yourself on the back, little Bobbie. Let others do that for you. It seems you've been getting quite a lot of that anyway—or were those pats on the backside?"

With great self-control Bobbie checked her temper. She knew it was useless to argue with the woman. She simply nodded her head and said, "Yes."

"Yes, what?" Hermani demanded.

"Yes, sir!" Bobbie saluted mockingly. "I've been sleeping with everybody in the newsroom. And as long as I continue to do so my job is secure. Is that what you want to hear?" Hermani glared at her and without further ado stormed out.

Bobbie was shaking but felt curiously relieved. At least she knew why Hermani detested her. Jerry had been right. It was jealousy—pure and unadulterated. What a hollow victory it must be for those successful women of Hermani's generation who with tremendous initiative and willpower had fought and scraped their way to the top against all odds, only to see, once they had achieved success, it given so easily to younger women for the asking. Times had changed. Qualified women could get many of the same jobs available to men. In the doing they robbed Hermani and those like her of their uniqueness. Hermani had made it in a "man's world," and her identity was all wrapped up in that achievement. No wonder she hated Bobbie, who had come in young and brash with nothing but a portfolio to recommend her for this job traditionally held by the male of the species.

Putting her shoulders back, Bobbie headed for her desk. That she understood Hermani now and even felt a little sorry for her would not make her nastiness any easier to take. But perhaps Bobbie could deflect that nastiness. Without thinking about it any further, she changed directions and headed for Hermani's office. The door was ajar so with a knock Bobbie entered. Without waiting for a greeting she plunged in.

"Hermani, please listen to me. I doubt that we'll ever be friends but let's not be enemies. I don't like to be enemies with people I admire and I really do admire you. You've made the Women's section of this paper a lot more than a list of wedding announcements. I know that several other papers in the country have followed your example and, well, I know you're a trailblazer. Nobody can take that away from you. I certainly can't."

The silence in the room was heavy.

135

"Nobody can call *you* a defeatist," Hermani said finally. "I still don't like you, but I'll tell you what: Keep out of my way as best you can and we'll coexist here. More than that I can't offer you."

"That will suit me just fine," Bobbie agreed. "I meant what I said before. You're quite a role model." Turning, she left as hastily as she had entered. Her smile, as she returned to her work, was self-satisfied. Her triumph was that not only did she do her work well but she was also learning to deal with people in an honest yet effective way. If only she had learned that a week ago in time to deal with the mayor, a small voice inside her head lamented.

Things were not clear in her mind. With her own eyes she had witnessed Dan looking at Sandra as only a man can look at a woman; she had seen the pictures of them leaving together for Washington. But perhaps she had misread the signals. For Dan could not have been lying to her when he had said all those things, when he had called her lovely and insisted that she was special. His words could not have been a form of bribery. He could not have been attempting to buy her cooperation with sweet nothings. Stifling a sob, she clenched and unclenched her fists. Could this agony be love? With all her will she had been trying to put Dan Allen out of her mind and out of her life with no success at all. She was as though possessed. But if it were love, then why did she feel it incumbent upon her to fight him at every turn? Why did she suspect him of the foulest motives and most villainous acts? Could it be because she felt that she was losing control? Or was it because she didn't think that plain Bobbie Schaeffer, who in her youth had spent too many a Saturday night at home washing her hair, could win the love of the glamorous, desirable, and powerful mayor of Milwaukee? And could it be that she feared the public scrutiny that such a liaison would naturally engender? Tongues wagging about a

136

blemish or a sagging chin or a skirt that hugged too tightly would be enough to send even the most self-confident of women running to their neighborhood shrink. Could Bobbie handle it? Indeed would she ever have the opportunity to test her mettle or was this worry about the limelight just another self-delusion to avoid facing the unpleasant truth that Dan Allen couldn't care less about her? Had he left willingly with Sandra on a political errand cum love tryst? Or had she chased him into Sandra's arms? Or perhaps his departure with Sandra was devoid of any meaning other than the obvious—the mayor's attorney accompanying him to an important meeting in her role as legal adviser. Perhaps this latest episode was but the last in a series of lovers' spats motivated by the green goddess, jealousy. She closed her eyes tight, for she felt herself floundering. She didn't know what the truth was.

She also didn't know how she was going to get through this week with the mayor out of town. When he got back, this whole matter would have to be resolved one way or the other. Let her take her cue from her confrontation with Hermani. Things left unsaid were always worse than the utterance. Were he to tell her he couldn't stand the sight of her, she would be devastated, but that devastation would surely be preferable to this uncertainty. Throwing her shoulders back, she decided to call him when he returned.

With that out of the way she tried to do some work. The piles of tickertape in the metal basket on her desk yielded no inspiration, and a familiar sense of urgency seized her. People in creative jobs lived in fear of the moment their muse would leave them, and each time they sat down with a blank mind, they felt that their careers were over. So it was for Bobbie that day and for the rest of the week. Blast Dan Allen and the hold he had over her!

CHAPTER XII

With a trembling hand she dialed Dan's home number—555-1160—numbers etched in her memory though she had never before dialed them. It was 7 A.M. on a Friday morning and she was sure he hadn't yet left for City Hall.

"Allen here" was his greeting as he picked up the phone. Her heart beat wildly at the sound of his voice. It was a voice both masterful and gentle. She hugged the phone to her ear.

"Hello," he said impatiently. "Who's there?"

"Hello, Dan."

"Bobbie! This is a surprise."

"Pleasant or unpleasant?"

"It's always nice to hear from you," he said coolly.

I shouldn't have phoned. What an idiot I am! she thought frantically.

"I was just calling to find out how your meeting went," she lied.

"I don't generally accept business calls before nine o'clock, but . . . It went well. They seemed convinced by my welfare-reform proposals. There—you have your scoop. Make a joke of it, if you can."

"That's not the reason I called," she said in a quavery voice. "I wanted to apologize for walking out on you without a word last Sunday." Bobbie was glad he couldn't

138

see the way she was clutching her sides with the phone cradled awkwardly between cheek and ear.

"*You* want to apologize?" he repeated incredulously. "That must be a Guiness book of firsts. To what do I owe this honor?"

"Forget it," she mumbled. "I shouldn't have called."

"You're always so hasty. But I must admit your instincts are good. Don't hang up. Tell me what you did all week."

"Worked, played, and had a marvelous time," she said smoothly, though she crossed the fingers of her left hand.

"Oh, did you find a new playmate?" he queried.

"You're the one with the playmate and probably with a whole hutch of bunnies to boot."

"If you're referring to my attorney, I find her very efficient and sweet of temper. You might take lessons from her."

"I think I prefer *your* teacher. Who was he, the Marquis de Sade or Machiavelli?"

"So you think I'm cruel and cunning," Dan chortled. "What better accolades for a politician? And I take it I'm living up to your opinion of me?"

"You're exceeding my expectations," Bobbie replied in a tightly controlled voice.

"That's good. I don't like to disappoint my constituents."

"Dan Allen, you are an impossible man. And let's just pretend this conversation never took place. I don't enjoy sparring at seven in the morning."

"Bobbie Schaeffer, *you* are an impossible woman. So that makes us well matched. And I've enjoyed this conversation. My wits needed sharpening for the hard day in front of me. What about lunch?"

"What about it?" Bobbie retorted hotly. "I'm bringing a peanut butter sandwich to work."

"Bon appétit," Dan said dryly. "And have a good day."

The buzz of the dial tone droned in her ear, yet Bobbie was reluctant to replace the receiver on the hook. Well, she had done it once again. And she had the unpleasant feeling that this had been her last chance to make amends. It didn't matter, she told herself furiously. It never could have worked out. That was that. And right now she'd do well to get on with the business of living.

The messenger boy dropped Bobbie's copy of the afternoon paper on her desk. The headlines jumped out at her. MAYOR HAS GOVERNOR AND SENATORS IN POCKET. The article called his trip an unparalleled victory for the conservatives and a personal triumph for the mayor. His support in the capital had increased and the polls showed an unprecedented amount of public support for his proposals. His political future was rosy indeed. Bobbie turned the page, finished the article with mixed feelings, and leafed through the rest of the sections. She stopped short at a small paragraph wedged in between the other tidbits in the City section. The article alleged that the mayor had been approached by an underworld crime boss. It went no further, not actually coming out and accusing the mayor of collusion, but the insinuation left a foul taste in Bobbie's mouth. With a start the thought occurred to her that maybe the same source who had leaked the story about C.J. had given Nesbitt this piece of information. The story said that the mayor and the gangster had met in an out-of-the-way, dark, smoky tavern. And dark, smoky taverns were not the sort of outpost where news reporters were generally placed. There were no reporters tailing Dan, so the information, if indeed it was true, had to have come from a source. Bobbie frowned and fought the inclination to phone Dan again and to warn him that he might be harboring a traitor in his inner circle. She didn't have to fight with herself for long because a mere forty-five minutes later her office phone rang and she picked it up to hear Dan's hello. Each time he spoke to her Bobbie reacted the same way. She felt, rather than heard, his voice. She thought of it as a velvet, soft and strong at the same time.

"Bobbie, my girl!" Dan said expansively. "What time do you get off work? Five?" Without waiting for affirmation he rushed on. "I want you to hurry home, feed your fish, and meet me at Joe's Diner on Roosevelt Boulevard and Lehigh."

"Why?" she said cavalierly. "I'm touched by your concern for my fish. But Joe's Diner? My fish might eat better!"

"You don't let me get away with anything, do you?" Dan laughed. "And what's wrong with Joe's Diner? After all, I'm a man of the people."

"It doesn't seem to be your style. Or has Joe recently employed strolling musicians?"

"No, but its red vinyl booths are very shiny."

"That settles it. I'll be there at five. But there is one thing: I thought we were mad at each other."

"No, we're mad *about* each other. You get my dander up, but in truth I haven't been able to stay mad at you for longer than, say, twenty minutes. And that's stretching it. You're too pretty."

"I think you need glasses."

"Not at all. That marvelous hook nose, those cross eyes, that fabulous wart on your chin, enrapture me."

"Very funny. But I must confess I feel the same way about your shiny bald head, your bulbous nose, and that splendid field of blackheads on your chin."

"It seems we're well suited for each other."

"Especially on Halloween," she said tongue-in-cheek.

"I don't have time to convince you of your beauty now," Dan said seriously, "but one day I'm going to hire

Scavullo to make a photographic portrait of you and I guarantee that you'll pass for a movie star. You have the features. I myself was surprised when I started meeting the so-called beauties of the world in person. They look no better than you or any pretty girl. When you see them in a film, it's after hours of makeup applied by the best makeup artist in the business, with the most suitable hairstyle and the finest clothes, in the most flattering lights and angle, and with all that each scene is shot about twenty times till these starlets look letter perfect. Believe me, you've got just as much potential as a Charlie's Angel."

"I'm convinced." Bobbie smiled happily into the phone. "Would you like to be my agent?"

"The offer is tempting, but I already have a job. I am available to fill another role in your life though."

"I don't think I will pursue that line now." Bobbie laughed nervously. "See you later, okay?"

Bobbie was puzzled. She sat for a long time looking at the black phone on her desk. Dan must have known about that article linking him with the underworld. His press relations staff got hold of the paper even before the paper's employees in the news building. Yet he hadn't mentioned it. Perhaps he felt it was too patently absurd to deserve even a word. She wondered if he made the connection with the story about C.J., figuring that the same person had leaked both accounts. If so, he must have known by now that Bobbie was innocent of the C.J. fiasco, for she could only have leaked the second story by inventing it. Smiling to herself, Bobbie became aware of a lightness in her breast that she had not felt for a long time.

CHAPTER XIII

Stepping out of her car, Bobbie glanced at the low gray building that was Joe's Diner. It was in a section of the city that in another two hours would be unsafe for a woman alone. As she walked gingerly amongst the broken glass and yellowed newspapers that littered the street, Bobbie thought this a strange place for a rendezvous with the mayor!

Her nose was assailed by the odor of Lysol and frying onions as she walked through the murky glass doors of Joe's Diner. The place was not crowded; she saw two or three men in shirt-sleeves bent over the gold-flecked Formica countertop. Only one of the booths that lined the wall was occupied. Her heart sank as she recognized Coleman as one of the occupants. Even Dan's big welcoming smile could not lift her spirits. She was in no mood to look at Coleman's dour face and put up with his rudeness. As she walked over to them her feet felt as if she had suddenly stepped into a pot of glue.

"Bobbie dear!" Dan's voice boomed as he slid over to make room for her.

"Good evening, gentlemen," Bobbie said in a soft, subdued voice. She was surprised to note that Coleman's lips were curled back over his pointy teeth in an imitation of a smile.

"It's nice to see you again, Bobbie."

Bobbie had trouble believing that those were really the words uttered in Coleman's nasal midwestern twang. She feared that her mouth had dropped open, for this was the first time Coleman had addressed her with anything remotely approaching civility. She was sorry she couldn't return the compliment.

"Have you been to any more baseball games?" Coleman asked.

"No, I haven't." She smiled weakly.

Dan excused himself to Bobbie and turning to Coleman spoke in a rapid, low staccato.

"Drive out to Runway Number One and have the fuel and engine rechecked. Post one of our men there and meet me back here in an hour with the car."

"Got it" was Coleman's short reply. Rising, he tipped his outmoded fedora at Bobbie and left. Bobbie looked after him in disbelief.

"To what do I owe that switch in attitude? Before, he acted like I was heading the most dangerous criminals list and now he's practically doing a soft shoe for my benefit."

"You have a charming flair for exaggeration," Dan admonished good-naturedly. "But you are right. In Coleman's eyes you are hereby exonerated of any attempts on my political life through the auspices of your newspaper and of any attempts to disarm me and temper my views under the guise of female adoration. In other words he no longer thinks you have been trying 'ɔ use me to learn my political secrets and thereby get ahead in your job. And I assume he's finally learned that no one can sway me from my purpose and my aspirations, not even my adorable dinner companion for this evening."

"Hmm, how do I answer that? The best way might be with another question. Why? And also, how? And now that I'm thinking of things to ask you, what are your political aspirations? I mean, you're the mayor already."

144

"What do you think of the title First Lady of Wisconsin?"

Bobbie gulped, "You jest, surely."

"Well, let's put off that discussion for a later date. Simply stated, my aspirations know no limit. And the why and how of Coleman is simple enough. He's found the real culprit upon whom to vent his rage and heap his scorn. You must have had an inkling that there was a Benedict Arnold in the ranks. I've long suspected the identity and just today had it confirmed."

"Don't keep me in suspense! Who is it?"

"It was Sandra."

Bobbie didn't say anything, though she wasn't surprised. The four dozen yellow roses Sandra had had sent to her had lodged like a thorn in her memory. A woman capable of so dastardly a deed, even in the name of unrequited love, would be capable of anything.

"Sandra is brilliant and beautiful, a prize by any standard," Dan continued explaining. "But she doesn't do it for me. I've always enjoyed working with her but those late nights at City Hall turned into something else. What can I say? Her kisses left me cold."

"You mean you've kissed her!" Bobbie pretended shock, though the kidding in her voice was evident. She noticed that she did feel a slight twinge at the thought of Dan embracing Sandra, even though she had long known about their one-time liaison.

"The two of us had quite a thing going for a short time. I ended it when I realized that it wasn't working out. The problem was that Sandra's perception was entirely different. She was falling in love with me or with the idea of me. That I'm the mayor of Milwaukee was an aphrodisiac for her. Power is like that."

"I thought oysters are like that," Bobbie said flippantly.

"Believe me, there's no aphrodisiac like power. She couldn't let go her hold and she couldn't accept the idea that she didn't turn me on." He laughed self-consciously. "When she saw you with me, she finally knew what the score was. You were standing in her way and she would do anything to get rid of you, including ruining my reputation and her career as the mayor's attorney. So she ingeniously planted the story about C.J., knowing that you would be the logical suspect. She also senses Coleman's aversion to you; she knows how he mistrusts anyone who reads anything more liberal than *Forbes* or *The Wall Street Journal*. It was clear to her that Coleman was only too ready to believe you were a fink and to use his influence to convince me of that. Her mistake was that she misjudged me. I pride myself on my insight and I think I know of what limits you're capable and of what fiendish ends she is capable. So in order to snare her in her own trap, I invented that little story about the underworld and me, let it slip when I knew she was listening, and made it plain that you knew about it. Of course you know nothing of the sort. I was not surprised when that piece appeared in today's paper."

Bobbie's head was reeling. Conflicting emotions warred with each other. On the one hand she was happy to be vindicated. She couldn't stand the thought that Dan harbored even the slightest doubt about her. On the other hand she didn't like his cavalier manipulation of the media. Deliberately allowing a false story to be published, even for the admirable end of ferreting out a skunk, was to do a disservice to not only the *Milwaukee Post* but to the press everywhere. In a halting voice that betrayed her emotions she expressed her thoughts to Dan. He listened, indicated his understanding, but answered her brutally.

"I'll be taking a beating from that story in the *Post* even with a printed retraction. It's similar to giving damaging evidence in court that is then disallowed. The jury is told to disregard what they've heard, but that's against human nature. There will always be some people who have read that article and ten years from now, if I'm running for president, will tell their friends and neighbors that I'm sitting in the pocket of the nation's hoods. One has to weigh evils. I've made my choice. Your good name was more important to me than a slight blemish on mine and on your newspaper's. And let's face facts. Newspaper reporting is not known for its accuracy. You people are always getting things wrong, whether it's an erroneous affidavit or the wrong shade of blue that a society lady was said to have worn.

"Sandra has been fired and she'll leave without a letter of recommendation. I only hope that the next fellow whom she sets her sights on is as wildly smitten as she or that he's smart enough not to mix business with romance."

"That's quite an earful," Bobbie said in a chastened voice. "I'm still not comfortable with what you did, and my boss is going to be furious. One thing is certain: You won't get the *Post*'s endorsement for reelection."

"I wouldn't have gotten it anyway," Dan said offhandedly. "You do what you have to do in this world and you take the consequences."

"To change the subject, Mr. Mayor, what are you going to do about this miserable neighborhood?"

"I didn't know I had a press conference scheduled," Dan grinned. "But in any case the answer is wrapped up with urban renewal and my program of tax incentives for industry in this city." Changing the subject, he asked, "What'll you have to eat anyway?"

"Maybe the waitress can recommend something."

"Let me order for you. The tomato soup and rice and grilled cheese sandwiches are superb."

"You're the gourmet," Bobbie acquiesced. "I take it then that you had an uncontrollable urge for a grilled cheese sandwich and would settle for nothing less than the best. Is that why we're dining in this inimitable style tonight?"

"That and the location and low profile of this place."

"It has a low profile all right, but what's so special about the location? Are you thinking of buying a house here? Or maybe of turning one of these buildings—that one across the street with the burned-out windows perhaps—into a condo? Condo conversion is getting big, you know."

Dan shook his head at her amusedly. "We're just two miles east of the airport. And if we approach it from this direction, we won't be seen."

"Why the secrecy? Are we playing cops and robbers? And why the airport?"

"Did you feed your fish?" Dan asked, ignoring her questions.

"I always listen to orders," Bobbie stated.

"Would you like to have a quiet weekend on a lake with nobody but me? No reporters, no aides, no police guards? Doesn't that sound great?" Dan asked enthusiastically.

"I guess so," Bobbie answered, hoping to strike the right note of casualness. Actually she felt like jumping up and down and cheering.

"I have a little cabin in Hayward that nobody knows about. It has bunk beds, an outhouse, and a well. And it has the most magnificent view this side of the Swiss Alps."

"I ought to stop home and pack some things. I'm not exactly dressed for the outdoors life." She looked down at her patent leather sling-back heels.

"Don't worry. The cabin's well equipped with sweat shirts, long underwear, and fishing tackle. There's a sport-

148

ing goods store in the town where we can pick up anything else you need."

Bobbie laughed giddily. "I might just be crazy enough to go along with you."

CHAPTER XIV

The Cessna's engines roared and the propeller whirled dizzyingly. Bobbie's stomach catapulted as she realized that this was her first time in a prop plane; the idea of it seemed terribly risky. The roar was deafening as takeoff became imminent. With a sidelong glance she studied Dan sitting behind the controls and looking cool and confident. His shirt sleeves were rolled up to reveal muscular forearms. Bobbie remarked to herself that even now when she feared death in a fiery plane crash she reveled in the sight of Dan's perfect body. A thoroughly modern woman in most respects, Bobbie refused to admit aloud that the thought of flying terrified her. That aerodynamics was a highly developed science she didn't deny. But it nevertheless seemed to her in her soul of souls that flying was unnatural. Well, if she had to die, at least it would be with her own true love.

"Stop being so nervous," Dan commanded with laughter in his voice.

"How did you know?"

"You're gripping the sides of your seat so tightly, your knuckles are white. And your mouth has a pinched look to it."

"Okay, Sherlock. I'm just a down-home girl who believes that man was meant to use the horse and buggy."

"Don't worry. I'm an ace pilot. Everything I do, I do well."

"So I've noticed."

"You haven't seen anything yet," Dan promised. Bobbie squirmed in the copilot's seat. Her head was thrown against the padded back as the plane rolled down the runway. She saw men with red flags waving signals to Dan. The airport terminal raced past her as the small plane gathered speed. The vibrations of the runway, without the cushioning that a big commercial plane provided, made her jaw feel as if a dentist's drill was grinding away at it. It was with relief that she sensed the plane lift off and begin its ascent. The tower, the houses and the roads beneath, quickly became smaller and smaller till they looked no bigger than a toy village.

"Not a bad takeoff," Bobbie commented. "Where did you learn to fly?"

"In the Air Force. I do some great tricks. Do you want to somersault?"

"No, thanks. I'll take your word for it. Anyway, if you did, I think those fellows tracking us on radar would have coronaries."

"That's probably true, and Coleman would undoubtedly be the first. He's up in the tower with them."

"Keeping tabs on you?"

"Yeah, he wants to make sure I don't defect to Chicago."

Bobbie laughed. "You seem so unmayorlike."

"What would you like me to do, bark orders at you? I'm a simple guy who likes to run things."

"What I would like you to do is stop looking at me and watch where you're flying."

"There's nothing up here but clouds. I've got a ten-mile clearance the entire route. That's one of the perks of office.

151

The only thing I could fly into is an angel and I don't have to, I have one sitting next to me."

"Oh, the seduction of Bobbie Schaeffer begins!"

"You're too smart for your own good," Dan guffawed. "Why couldn't I fall in love with a dumb blonde?"

Instead of answering Bobbie looked out, mesmerized at the cloud formation they entered. It seemed to her that they were flying through a cotton-candy world, complete with castles, turrets, and lagoons.

The trip took no more than an hour and before they knew it, Dan was telling her to brace herself for the landing. The needles on the myriad dials of the instrument panel were jumping back and forth, and Bobbie, aware of her lack of mechanical skill, marveled that Dan along with his other accomplishments could fly this aircraft. That the landing was too bumpy to meet his standards Bobbie knew from the grim set of his mouth, but she was nonetheless impressed, for she knew that the only way she could ever be induced to fly a plane was with a gun pointed at her head.

No sooner had the plane rolled to a halt than a white truck with white-suited technicians drove up to them in order to wheel a portable landing ramp up to the plane. Bobbie stepped through the open cockpit door and was met by a smiling man unrolling a tattered red carpet before them.

"I thought the purpose of this weekend was anonymity." Bobbie winked.

"That was one of two aims," Dan said, shrugging resignedly. "Perhaps I'll have better luck with the other one."

"You'll have to wait and see, won't you?" Bobbie said sweetly.

At the end of the ramp Bobbie and Dan were greeted with a cream and green Dodge in which two porcine-looking town officials waited with plastic smiles. Dan grabbed Bobbie's arm and shoved her in the opposite direction.

"Run," he commanded.

Bobbie ran. Dan steered her around the low arrivals building to the front of the terminal where what Bobbie guessed was Hayward's only cab sat at curbside. They jumped in and Dan snapped an address to the driver.

"That would rank as an undignified departure," Bobbie commented with raised eyebrows.

"I know, I know," Dan groaned. "It was unpolitic. But I simply won't go through any formalities now. This is a personal weekend and I'm sorry if I had to offend anyone but those officials ought to have more tact. I refuse to put up with people nosing in on the little time I take for myself."

Bobbie leaned over and kissed him on the cheek. "I second the motion. Are we heading straight for the cabin or should we lay in some supplies first?"

"You're right. Driver, take us into town first, the Army-Navy store."

With a disconcerted expression on his face, for he feared recognition, Dan escorted Bobbie into the Army-Navy store, where she bought, in record time, sneakers, jeans, underwear, and a toothbrush. The next stop was the local market, where they left laden with bags of T-bone steaks, eggs, tomato juice to mix with the vodka Dan assured her was in plentiful supply at the cabin, French bread, and a fresh pineapple. And that Dan assured her was for only one meal. He would phone in his order for the rest of the weekend once they were settled. The cab, meter ticking, was waiting and the driver jumped out to help them with their packages. As the taxi sped along the spruce-lined roads, Bobbie breathed deeply of the fresh country air.

With all the talk of pollution and spoiled resources she had lost sight that places like this still existed.

Dan's cabin was made of logs and was in its rough-hewn, rustic way perfect. It had exposed beams, a loft, a potbellied stove, and hand-braided cotton rugs on the floor.

"I love it! Let's stay here forever!"

"Wait till you see the view. Come over here." Dan beckoned her over to the single modern touch—a bay window. It looked out on a medium-sized lake, tranquilly shimmering in the setting sun like a diamond held up to the light. Small islands, some so small they were mounds of dirt with a tree or bush, dotted the lake, lending it a picture-postcard prettiness. Bobbie spotted a canoe and a sailboat moored to a rickety private pier.

"Are they yours?"

"They're my pride and joy."

"Boy! A pilot, a yachtsman—"

"And an Indian chief," Dan finished.

"But not a thief?" she teased.

"Haven't I stolen your heart?"

"Just my sanity," Bobbie teased. "But in an insane world it's crazy to be sane."

"My little philosopher," Dan murmured. "I think a little whirl around the lake would do you good. It'll put you in the right frame of mind for the weekend."

"Can't I at least change my shoes?"

"Go ahead. I'll wait down at the lake."

Quickly changing into sneakers, sweat shirt, and jeans, Bobbie laughed giddily. She was happier to be here in this cabin smelling of spruce than she would be anywhere in the world, Monte Carlo and the Taj Mahal included. As she walked to the door she paused to look out the window. There was Dan poised against the mast of his boat staring out at the sun's last crescent glowing a dull red as it

154

finished its descent over the horizon. That ever a man was born who could set a woman's heart so afire Bobbie doubted. She, who all her life had possessed the ultimate in sangfroid when it came to romance, was now quivering like a lamb going to slaughter. Standing there, his strong profile and lean straight physique etched against the purple-hued sky, he looked like a god landed by mistake on this earth. How she had been so singled out by this best of men she didn't want to know; at this moment she only wanted to thank her stars for her good fortune. With an effort she pulled herself away from the sight of him and ran down to join him.

"You look fetching in that outfit," he said as he pulled the sweat shirt's hood onto her head. "Like a pixie."

"And pixies follow the rainbow to find the pot of gold at the end," she said, smiling. "So let's go!"

"I've already found my pot of gold." Dan put his arm around her.

"What you've found is the alchemist's secret of changing lead into gold," she corrected.

"You give me too much credit. At the very most I found the key to unlock the treasure buried in your heart." Bobbie blushed. "Have you sailed before?" he asked.

"No, but I'm game."

"I'll hold off on lessons till tomorrow. For now you can sit and enjoy the ride. Just duck when I tell you to or the boom will knock off your head."

"That wouldn't be a very auspicious start to the weekend," Bobbie said solemnly. "How about if I just lie at the bottom of the boat the whole time?"

"Now don't go overboard," Dan admonished. "Ho, ho," he laughed mockingly, "did you get it?"

"That was vaguely humorous," Bobbie pronounced dryly, "but you know what? It's a good thing you're not trying to get a job writing for *The Muppet Show*."

"One of the best things about you is that you'll never let me get conceited," Dan said, pulling Bobbie against his chest. But he pushed her away almost immediately. "If we're going for that sail, we'd best not get sidetracked."

Smooth as glass, the water rippled in tiny concentric circles as the boat cut through it. Dan handled the dinghy easily, always catching the wind as its direction changed with only the slightest movement of his hand. Preferring the security of knowing she was in his hands, Bobbie demurred when he offered her the rudder. She closed her eyes and concentrated on the breeze rushing against her cheeks and the water gently lapping against the boat. She thought it a shame that people allowed their lives to be inundated with trivia when there were beautiful moments like this to cherish. She hoped that in the future, when the Hermanis of this world bothered her, this night and others like it would provide her with the resources to rise above their pettiness.

"Dan," she whispered.

"Yes?"

"I'm hungry." Bobbie bit her lip in vexation. That wasn't what she meant to say but somehow those three little words that were on the tip of her tongue could not be uttered. Feisty she had been called many a time. Stubborn jackass would be more appropriate, she thought, for she still could not say aloud the words that would show her to be warm, vulnerable, and needing like the rest of humanity.

"The grilled cheese didn't hold you, eh? We'll rustle up a couple of steaks when we get back. See that little island over there?" He pointed to a patch of earth no bigger than twenty feet square rising out of the lake. "Once, about five years ago, I spent a week alone on that place. I wanted to prove to myself that I could do it."

"So you played at Robinson Crusoe."

156

"Not quite. I had a canoe there, plenty of food and water, and a sleeping bag. It was the most important time of my life because I found what I was made of and I liked it. I found that I had guts and energy and mettle and I learned that I could go all the way in this world, as far as I chose. That's when I decided to run for mayor and from there, who knows, maybe I'll go for governor."

"I hope you get what you want."

"I know I will," Dan replied.

As she saw the steely glint in his eye, even in the dusk, she knew he was right. No one could stop him. She shivered.

CHAPTER XV

"Drat! We're out of salt!" Dan tossed the empty plastic saltshaker into the sink. He surveyed his rare steak in frustration.

"I saw some A-1 Sauce in the refrigerator. Should I get it?" Bobbie asked anxiously.

"No." He attacked his saltless steak voraciously. Bobbie could tell by the way his eyebrows were knit that he was annoyed with himself for having overlooked something, be it so insignificant a thing as salt. Living with a perfectionist, if that was ever to pass, could prove a problem for someone like herself, Bobbie thought. Though she excelled in her work she was by her very nature disorganized, as anyone peering into her clothes closets or dresser drawers could readily bear witness. But, she sighed, she wasn't married to him and she thought she could fake neatness for a weekend at least.

"Milwaukee is turning into a city of suburban malls," Dan said unexpectedly. "I'm going to turn it around. What do you think of a summerfest downtown with different attractions every night and a permanent crafts and antiques fair?"

"It should draw people into the city," Bobbie said. She was puzzled. Here she had thought he was brooding about the empty saltshaker and it turned out he was planning a summerfest! "But where are you going to get the financing?"

"It'll pay for itself in the end and with the added trade in town it shouldn't be too difficult to convince businessmen to buy short-term municipal bonds. Milwaukee has a good rating."

"Why don't you file away that subject for Monday morning?" Bobbie suggested. She rose to walk behind his chair. Gently she pressed her fingers around his temples in slow, sensuous circles. The tips of her fingers as they touched his olive skin were charged as though by a tiny electric current. She knew it was her imagination but still the effect was not lessened. He pulled her around and into his lap. Their eyes were level now and as he stared into her eyes; she found herself drowning in the limpid depths of his orbs and wishing with all her might that he would avert his gaze, for she had not the strength to do so. She was not to be spared; he held her locked for an eternity. . . .

He broke the silence at last. "Come to bed." Bobbie's head was reeling. She had experienced two fiascos with him. Dare she tempt the fates once more? Of course she had no choice in the matter. She went with him, and when he kissed her, she knew, as she had always known, that she was his, totally and forever. She curled onto the bed and with her clothes on watched him this time as he slowly unbuttoned his shirt. His unflinching gaze was on her lips as he finished with his shirt and stepped out of his pants. Naked, he knelt to kiss her hand and slipped into bed beside her. Bobbie lay rigid as embarrassment—for she felt as though she had played this scene before—washed over her. Sensing her confusion, Dan kissed her tenderly. He caressed her slowly and whispered to her. His mouth was hungry upon hers. With tender hands he undressed her easily.

159

As Bobbie felt her flesh quiver against his, she knew that she had to open herself to this man. Aware of her willingness, Dan entered her. He guided her; he was gentle with her. Bobbie tensed with the first sharp pain but relaxed as it melted into a voluptuous sweetness. All the feelings that had wrenched her heart these past few weeks, jealousy, desire, denial, rejection, were consumed in the full-blown intensity of love fulfilled. Finally drained, yet curiously complete, she fell asleep with her head nestled against her lover's chest, her arms encircling him.

The next morning, as they sipped their coffee, there passed between them a special look that was even more intimate than the gropings of the night before. Dan picked out fishing tackle and bait and together they paddled out in the silver canoe. With infinite patience Dan taught her how to fly cast and with his finger to his lips, cautioning her to silence, he would quietly correct her mistakes. After a while Bobbie began to get the feel of the rod and to enjoy throwing her line out as far as she could. She hadn't caught any fish, though the sun was almost midway up the sky, and Dan had thrown back all of his for they were too small for his sporting sense. When her bait began to bob up and down in the water, so accustomed was she to the scarcity of action, it almost escaped her notice. With a jerk her fishing rod almost fell out of her hands. She pulled back sharply in a reflex action and reeled in frantically; she almost fell over as she saw a large-mouth bass dangling from the end of her line, whipping its body back and forth in a frenzied effort to free itself. On the one hand she was almost moved to let go of the line and allow the fish to go free, for it fought valiantly for its life. On the other hand she was overwhelmed with the heady sensation of her first catch, of *the* first catch of the day, and she jerked up again with all her might. Along with the bass she landed on the floor of the canoe. The first slappings of its tail against the aluminum bottom of the boat were drowned out by Dan's whoops of joy.

"That's an eight pounder at least," he chortled. "You've worked for your supper, girl."

Bobbie laughed happily. "I always land big fish." She blew him a kiss. With one quick movement Dan disengaged the hook from the fish's mouth.

"Shall we fry you or bake you, Mr. Bass?" Bobbie asked her catch.

"As long as you use plenty of butter and lemon, it's all the same for me," Dan spoke up.

"You're not sexist, are you? I mean you *are* going to help me cook?"

"Division of labor. I was intending to clean it, but if you'd rather switch, it'll be my pleasure," Dan answered with a twinkle in his eye.

"Okay, okay, tell me where you keep the aprons," Bobbie acquiesced.

"In another couple of hours. The fish won't spoil and maybe I'll be as good a fisherman as you. You have to give me a chance. Here, let me put another lure on your line." He took a red plastic lure out of his bag and threaded it through her hook. "This is a special Japanese lure. You could catch a whale with that." No sooner had she cast her line into the water than she felt a strong tug.

"I think I just did. You have to help me with this one."

Dan reeled in the rod and jumped behind her. Even with the two of them pulling and heaving, the fish engaged them in an awesome struggle. Dan gave it some slack, played the line, and with a mighty heave managed to get it up and land it with a smack next to the bass.

"This is beginner's luck," he explained, shaking his head ruefully.

"It's true talent. If I ever get tired of cartooning, I'll buy a fishing boat and start my own business." Bobbie grinned.

"You'll have to develop your biceps first. I'll buy you some body-building equipment for Christmas," Dan said. "Not that your body needs building," he added as an afterthought. "In fact it's perfect the way it is. And anyway, I doubt if you'll ever tire of cartooning."

"You're right there," Bobbie admitted. "How do you like this one? Picture yourself hooked on my line, plopped in the bottom of the boat."

"And the name of your boat is the *Milwaukee Post,* right?" Dan smiled. "No, thanks. I think I prefer some of your other cartoons. You've never really explained to me how you got interested in cartooning. It's an unusual profession, I always thought. But knowing you, I have come to see that you couldn't have chosen a better field. It suits your personality."

Bobbie smiled. "I'm glad you understand that. I never could explain my job to anybody. It's only the people who know me well who realize that there's nothing else I could have done. I draw what I see. As far as I'm concerned it's real life that I'm drawing, even if real life doesn't think so. If people think my cartoons are loony and wild, it's only because that's how my mind is."

"I know that. And the joke's on everybody else because you're making money doing something you enjoy and being yourself. That's the mark of a successful person. And success is exceedingly attractive." Dan paused and swallowed hard. "Bobbie, I don't know how to say this— and I'm rarely at a loss for words—but I don't meet too many women whom I feel are my equal. And going to bed with a blond bombshell who speaks in one-syllable words is not my idea of a good time. Last night was unique in my experience."

"An experienced man is like good Scotch: mellow, smooth—" she cut in.

"It's not necessary to find humor in everything!" Dan said severely.

"As I was saying . . ." he continued. "Oh, hell! You've killed my mood. Why can't you listen and bat your eyelashes when you're supposed to?"

"You just got through telling me how nice it was to make love to an equal and now you're telling me to bat my eyelashes!" she flared. "Men! You're all schizophrenic! Anyway, we're not equal. I'm the one who caught these fish, remember?"

Dan laughed but looked at her with serious eyes. "I want you to marry me."

To say that Bobbie felt tears of joy springing to her eyes and that her heart soared would be to understate. "Do you mean that?" she whispered ecstatically.

"No, it's an April fool's joke," Dan teased. "Of course I mean it. I can't think of anyone else I would rather share my life with. That is, if you can stand a temperamental and occasionally autocratic mate."

"Temperamental, yes; autocratic, no. I'll keep a cot in my office for the times you're being dictatorial." She looked up in alarm. "You wouldn't want me to quit my job?"

"Of course not! Your job is you. And you'll run your life as you see fit. The only thing I wouldn't want you to do is run for mayor on the opposite ticket or become a stripper!"

"No fear of that!" Bobbie looked ruefully down at her somewhat flat chest. "Oh, Dan!"

"You haven't said yes yet," Dan interjected.

"Haven't I? I suppose I thought you could read my mind. Yes, yes, yes, yes, yes, yes." She threw her arms around him and waited for his kiss. It was a sweet kiss, strong yet tender. It was a kiss that made promises that words could not tell. As he pulled away Bobbie sat quietly contemplating their tomorrows, the lake, the bass at her feet, and her good fortune.

"We smell fishy," she said finally, twitching her nose.

"You always find the right way to break a silence." Dan laughed.

With steady, quick strokes he paddled back to the pier. After stringing the two fish together (the second was even larger than the first), he carried them behind the cabin where he cleaned and fileted them. Bobbie fried a couple of filets for lunch and they both agreed that it was the best fish they had ever eaten. Like carefree children they talked and laughed over lunch. Afterward, using the need for digestion as an excuse for inactivity, they strolled down to the lake, where they lay in the bottom of the canoe, side by side, fingers intertwined, the afternoon sun warming them as the lake rocked them into a state of quietude.

They didn't fish the rest of the day, nor the next. They spent the time in conversation. They shared their deepest thoughts, their fears, their secret pleasures. Dan told her about the time he had fulfilled a childhood fantasy and gone to Chicago to appear as a standup comic at the Improvisation, a nightclub that drew its biggest crowd on amateur nights. Thoroughly chagrined, he had been booed and jeered off the stage in less than five minutes. Bobbie told him about the time she had run for class officer in college and gotten two votes! They laughingly concluded that it was for the best that he had forged his career in politics and she had forged hers in humor.

They spent much of the weekend walking along the rocky shore and skimming stones across the water. Through it all was woven the fabric of delight they found in each other's presence.

On Sunday morning Dan led her on a trek through the woods. Brambles scratched her arms and she noticed an abundance of poison ivy along the way. It ended abruptly, giving way to a small pine forest, cool and clean, though dank with the smell of moss—a refreshing contrast to the wild undergrown area they had traversed. Together they remarked on the play of sunlight through the leaves and on the musical song of the birds. The trees, tall and slender, made Bobbie feel diminutive and excited as if, like Gretel of the fairy tale, she was about to come upon a gingerbread house. What Dan led her to was even better. As they came to the other end of the tiny forest they stepped out into the sun and were confronted with an area of foliage so thick, it was almost a wall. Parting the prickly bushes for her, Dan motioned her through. Bobbie gasped in delight as she gazed openmouthed at three natural pools placed like steps on different levels. A waterfall fell like a curtain from the upper pool, causing the sparkling water to trickle like so many liquid crystals to the other two pools below. The entire enclave was surrounded by lush greenery and wild flowers, giving it an air of intimacy and unreality.

Wordlessly Dan pulled her under a magnolia tree heavy with pink flowers. With a gentle movement he lifted her chin so their eyes met in a charge of electric recognition. Together they sank to the dewy grass. A man who loved woman, he explored and reveled in her body till she shuddered with the abandonment of pure pleasure. As he kissed her hair, her eyes, her mouth, her breasts, Bobbie writhed with hitherto unknown flames of passion tingling her insides and making her pull him closer to her. Happy in the embrace of his powerful arms, she knew that she never wanted him to let her go, that she could hold the moment of meeting between his soft lips and hers in infinity! He made love to her again and again, choreographing his movements to her natural rhythm. What he wrested from her then was not only her body but her soul.

Bobbie had always heard that time flew when you were

having fun, but she found the opposite to be true. Having reveled in and cherished each moment of the weekend, she felt as if it had stretched into weeks. Each moment of the two days was etched into her consciousness, so unlike the oblivious state in which she often passed time. Time slowed down for them, almost as if a projector were rolling a film at the wrong speed. And she was glad, for she didn't want the film to be over.

During the flight back to Milwaukee Dan asked her if she wanted to take the controls.

"No, thanks. I can hardly believe I'm sitting in this little plane as a passenger. You're the only person who could get me on so small a craft."

"You show good judgment," Dan said, patting her thigh.

Bobbie pulled back. "Please, just concentrate on flying." She paused. "By the way, are all Republicans such good lovers?"

"Sure. It comes with party membership—ten easy lessons. But you flaming liberals aren't too bad in bed either. I hope it doesn't come from practice."

"It's instinctive—with the right person."

"What?"

"I said it's instinctive," she shouted over the roar of the engines as the plane started a steep climb.

"You have the right instincts!" Dan shouted back. "I'm off to Madison tomorrow. Can you come?"

"What?" It was Bobbie's turn to ask.

"Never mind." They lapsed into silence as the noise in the cockpit became deafening. An unexpected squall had developed over Milwaukee and a downdraft caused the plane to lose a hundred feet too quickly for comfort. The set of Dan's face was grim as he manipulated the controls. Though she knew she ought to be frightened, Bobbie was calm. If anybody could see this through, it was Dan and

166

she knew he would. Her trust was not misplaced and it was not lost on Dan. As the plane rolled to a successful halt and the tension drained out of his face, Dan turned to her.

"My mother is going to love you."

"And I'm going to love her for having produced you," Bobbie replied.

There was no more time for conversation; Coleman was waiting at the runway for Dan with a bulging briefcase and a nonstop stream of talk. It was incredible that so much could happen in one little weekend—and the way Coleman behaved it all seemed to be of earth-shaking importance. He had greeted Bobbie cordially again, resigned to the idea that he might be seeing a lot more of her in the future. There were two cars at the airport. The other was to bring Bobbie home. With precious little ado, Dan bid Bobbie good-night and, giving Coleman all his attention, sped off into the night. The magic of the weekend was broken.

CHAPTER XVI

The magic was about to be smashed to smithereens, for no sooner had she slammed the car door in front of her apartment than she was accosted by Sandra who, like a harbinger of the night, had been lurking in the shadows of Bobbie's street awaiting her return.

"Good evening," Sandra hissed.

Bobbie jumped and whirled to face her. As she stared at the beautiful brunette whose face was covered with fury and twisted with derisiveness, she wished ardently that it had been a mugger who had accosted her.

"What can I do for you, Sandra?" Bobbie asked nervously.

"It's what I can do for you," Sandra glowered. "Out of the kindness of my heart I'm going to tell you a tale and perhaps spare you the same hell that I've been through."

"Why would you do that?" Bobbie asked suspiciously.

"Let's just say that I'm doing it in the spirit of sisterhood. Women have to stick together. Can we go up to your apartment and talk?"

"I'd rather not," Bobbie answered quickly. "I have been cooped up so long, I'd like to get some fresh air."

"All right, you don't want me in your apartment. I can understand that. After all, we know the same man—and I mean 'know' in the biblical sense—so you want your apartment unsullied by my presence. You want to keep some part of your life private. Am I getting close?"

"I don't know what you're talking about, Sandra, and I think I prefer to keep it that way. Excuse me." She moved toward the door of her town house. With feline grace Sandra jumped in front of her, barring her way.

"You don't understand. I'm not trying to hurt you. I'm trying to help. We're sisters."

"Cut it out. You're not my sister, genetically, politically, or in any other way."

"Granted. We don't look alike." Sandra laughed, snidely tossing her shiny black mane. "But we both know opportunity when we see it, as does our mutual friend. He's going to get a lot of good ink out of his liaison with you and don't think he's not aware of it. The darling of the *Milwaukee Post* and the big bad Republican mayor. All the brouhaha that your paper makes of everything he does is reduced to a lot of hot air when the liberal's liberal falls in love with him. Mayor Dan is smart, and if he can satisfy his hunger at the same time he's rendering your paper impotent in its opposition to him, don't think he won't seize the chance. And in bed he brings out the best in his women. Don't I know!"

An angry retort was upon Bobbie's lips when she flashed back to the conversation she and Dan had had aloft in his plane. She had taken his compliment of her performance as flattery, but maybe— She was a fool to listen to anything this woman had to say! "Hell hath no fury like a woman scorned," she thought. Sandra was the living proof. "You're making a fool of yourself, Sandra."

"I've already been made a fool of. You're next," Sandra spat out. "I wouldn't be lurking on dark streets, waiting for a milk-fed cornflower-complexioned girl to come skipping home if I didn't believe what I was saying. Don't

169

trust Dan. He has a track record to make Casanova look like a Trappist monk.

"And where is he now? With his trusted aide? You ought to know that dear Coleman has several functions, one of which is to scout out companions for a quick midnight release when our mayor has been working too hard. You didn't know that, did you?"

Bobbie paled. "As an attorney, you would, I think, be a bit more circumspect with your accusations. I think a court of law would consider them slanderous."

"They'll never get to a court, will they?" She clucked her tongue pityingly. "You're so far gone, you refuse to see the truth. You're being used like I was used and like someone else will be used. Dan doesn't know what love is. He has no time for it. He's a politician, remember? And he's single-minded and obsessed with power. The thing about politicians is that they're public men with no multifaceted inner man buried under the facade. Dan is just what he appears to be on television: a smiling, handsome wheeler-dealer—a phony."

"You're a sick woman, Sandra! I knew it when you had Dan's roses sent here, and you're displaying it again." Bobbie pushed her aside and ran up the steps to her entranceway.

"Did he tell you about the time he flopped as a standup comedian?" Sandra taunted the retreating Bobbie. "Did he?"

An arrow could not more painfully have pierced Bobbie's heart. That he had confided the same thing to Sandra lent her ugly accusations a credence that had till this moment been lacking. With clammy hands she gripped the mahogany bannister leading up to her apartment. Turning around, she saw Sandra watching her in the eerie light of the streetlamp, with a cruelly triumphant smile playing around the corners of her mouth. All of the old insecurities that Bobbie had worked so hard to defeat came bubbling up to the surface of her psyche, mimicking Sandra's venomous words. Why indeed, she tormented herself, would Dan fall in love with her? Sandra was a beauty queen. Bobbie would not have been eligible even to enter the contest. That Dan had explained and justified his feelings about her was beside the point. Her own feelings of inadequacy, stemming from childhood, could not be stilled. It all came back to the feeling that she was not beautiful, that many people saw her as average-looking. Indeed she saw herself as average-looking. It was said that people were wont to choose mates who were roughly comparable to themselves in looks. So why would Dan choose her? She looked more like his research assistant than his fiancée. And even if it were true that he loved her, would she have the fortitude to withstand all the spitefulness that would be directed against her? The press, at least the fashion columns, would make mincemeat of her. She knew what things cost in the world of politics. If she looked particularly frowsy in one picture, it would cost Dan twenty votes. If it came out that Larry and Jerry, her two good friends, were homosexuals, it would cost him a thousand votes. Who needed it? And would she be able to ignore the barbs and arrows? Here she had been confronted with one person who had a vested interest in hurting her and Dan, and yet she had not the ability to shake off the hurtful words like so much dirt.

Snapping out of her reverie, she walked shakily to the top of the stairs, inserted her key in the lock, and with a sigh told herself that this was not going to work. It was a mistake. Either Sandra was right and Dan was a louse, or Bobbie was going to blow it, for she had not the makings of a politician's wife. She was simply too weak for the job. She longed for the simplicity of her life before she met Dan. That had been a content Bobbie, happy with herself,

171

with her job, with the business of living. She hadn't wanted anything more, hadn't been looking for complications. It was Dan who had pushed himself into her life. She had always entertained the disturbing thought that she was not fated for marriage because she was simply too prickly and intractable to maintain a relationship with a man. Even her own mother had said on numerous occasions that she was stubborn as a mule and that she pitied the poor man who eventually ended up with her.

What had gone wrong? The weekend had been a fantasy. And now she felt all the pains of Woman Betrayed. Dare she trust Sandra? It was easy to understand that Sandra could be making this all up. But how could she know about Dan's failure as a comic unless he had confided in Sandra as he had confided in her? Through her pain Bobbie could see the clever, diabolical nature of Sandra's story. But it didn't matter, for Bobbie sensed a core of truth at its bottom. She wondered with a sickening ache what the dark, alluring lawyer was like in bed but attempted to squelch the thought. She did not succeed.

Her head throbbing from suppressed emotion, Bobbie moved to her bedroom, where she lay down on her bed. She curled her legs up to her chest and with her arms she encircled the pillow. Then the tears started. First there was a trickle meandering down her nose and soon after a torrent. Sobs racked her body and she moaned like a wounded animal. As high as the euphoria of the weekend, so deep was her grief now. She was a person who needed balance. She was not made to fluctuate between high and low, between trust and doubt, between love and despair. Perhaps Dan could explain away every one of Sandra's accusations. But wouldn't there be Louisas and Susans and Alices to worry about next time? Wouldn't there be campaign trails to compete with and ambition to which she would play second fiddle? Wouldn't there be her career to juggle against his, and her need for privacy to war against a public avidly curious about their politicians and their politicians' wives? In the hot passion of a courtship it was all Dan could do to sneak away for one weekend. She needed more from her man or she needed nothing at all.

That it had been so good with Dan made the knowledge that she would have to be without him all the more terrifying. In a moment of lucidity she asked herself why, when she had come so close to happiness, did she flee. She was afraid, but were her fears justified? When you had nothing, you had nothing to lose. And when you had everything, a great and wonderful love, you risked not only the loss of that love but the loss of yourself. The answers were easy. She was an insightful woman. But that didn't make it any easier for her. She knew how hard it would be to forget him, for when she would not be seeing his face in newspapers or on the television screen, she would be seeing his face in her mind's eye.

She wondered what a child of Dan's would look like, and with the thought there rose in her a terrible yearning. She would have wanted his child. In her despair her stomach churned, her heart ached; she cried until her mouth dried and her eyes became narrow red slits. Still sobbing, she fell finally into a heavy sleep, with all her clothes still on except for her sneakers, which she had worn back from the lake and which lay, still caked with mud, on her furry white rug.

CHAPTER XVII

The next morning, filled with determination, for she knew what was best, Bobbie typed a letter to Dan. She told him what he had meant to her, how wonderful it had been with him. But she also said that life had to be lived from the head and not from the heart. She told him that he and his life-style were too rich for her blood. She needed liverwurst, and he was pâté de foie gras. She also told him about Sandra. Not wanting to put the letter through the office mails, she walked with it to the corner mailbox. It was only through the sheer force of her will that she succeeded in putting it through the slot, for as she pressed her lips to its seal, the letter seemed almost to stick to her mouth. Having written and mailed what she saw as her last good-bye, she thought she would feel relieved. Instead she felt burdened by the dreadful feeling that she had just ruined her only chance for happiness. She would have to work on those feelings.

Days passed. Then weeks. Dan didn't call. Bobbie was not surprised, though she could not honestly say she was glad. There was just so much gaff any man could take. She assumed also that he saw the ultimate reasonableness of her good-bye. Or perhaps, she thought with a twisted smile, he had found someone else. Perhaps Milwaukee's other newspaper had just hired an attractive editor. Who knew? What did surprise Bobbie was that her pain did not abate. Indeed, though she rarely spoke of it to anyone, it appeared to her to increase in intensity. As early summer passed into late summer, and late summer into autumn, Bobbie learned to live with that pain—it was her constant companion.

Larry and Jerry were the only people who knew what had happened with Dan, and like the best of friends, they tried their hardest to make her forget. Bobbie feared she was getting fat, for two or three times a week they would bring a pepperoni pizza to her office and, seated around it on the floor, would not let her get away without eating her share.

"Do you want the real story on the Drips?" Larry asked one day.

"You mean the rock group that almost caused a teen riot downtown last week?" Bobbie asked.

"The very same. Not too many people know their origins. Are you ready?"

"Ready."

"They all met in London at a therapy group for bed wetters. The therapist didn't help them with their incontinence, but they did find out they sang well together. So three years later we find them giving sell-out concerts, making gold records, signing autographs, and wetting beds around the world."

Bobbie's sides were splitting. "You're weird! And stop making me laugh or I'm going to have to join that group!"

Larry leaned back on the floor, supported by his elbows. He was beaming. Bobbie knew it was because she had laughed, because he had made her forget for a little while. He was a dear friend.

Almost every day Jerry or Larry would pop a head around the corner of her office door and tell her a joke. Most of the jokes were awful; she couldn't imagine where they had dug them up. But Bobbie always laughed, more from the tenderness her friends inspired in her than from their humor. It was odd. Friendships could be solid, constant. You could have fun with your friends. You could confide in them. You could even trust some friends with your life. Yet friends, even triple-A-rated friends, could not fill the aching need that throbbed in Bobbie's bosom. She had tried, with a surgeon's quick thrust, to cut out her heart. What she had ended up with was an executioner's song, for there were too many days that rang like a dirge in her ears.

One morning as she was hammering away at the keys of her banged-up manual typewriter (the electrics were saved for the reporters), Cal Nesbitt knocked at the door of her office.

"Morning, Bobbie. Do you have a minute or two?"

"Why, of course, Cal. I'm just writing a letter. Sit down." Bobbie hadn't decided consciously to start calling Nesbitt by his first name, it had slipped out naturally some time after that ill-fated last weekend with Dan. She had come to a sort of intrinsic understanding with herself that she was as adult as anybody of her parents' or even her grandparents' generations. She had adult problems and she had adult skills. And she saw no reason to place herself in a position of servility and someone else in a position of power by addressing them by a surname when they called her Bobbie.

"I have some good news for you." Cal paused dramatically. "I'm going to let you have a shot at doing the Sunday Editorial Page cartoon."

"Why, Cal, that's wonderful! Thank you! But what about the regular syndicated cartoon? Will we run together?"

"I'm going to suspend the syndicated cartoon for a while. After all, why call in a caterer when I've got my

176

own pastry chef sitting right here? I don't have to tell you how pleased I am with your work."

"You don't"—Bobbie grinned—"but I wouldn't mind hearing it!"

"I'm not going to be the one to give you a swelled head." Cal Nesbitt smiled avuncularly. "But I will say that *your* work has vindicated *me*. I had to put up with a great deal of flak when I hired you."

"Hermani?" Bobbie asked.

"No. Hermani was the least of my worries, though the most outspoken. There were grumblings throughout the paper. You were the first rookie assigned to an important position here. One of the reasons we're a first-rate paper is that we've got an experienced staff—all tried and true, with impressive credentials and glossy portfolios."

"Why *did* you hire me, Cal?" Bobbie asked with bated breath.

"I followed a hunch. You came to my office with virtually no credentials and the mangiest portfolio, but I saw something in your rough cartoons. It was a rare sense of authenticity. Your work was fresh and honest. And I saw something in your eyes: I saw that you were driven. You reminded me of myself at your age. I wasn't wrong, was I?"

"I hope not," Bobbie said. "I wouldn't mind following in your footsteps, being as successful a cartoonist as you are an editor."

Nesbitt looked ashen. "I'm quite an editor, aren't I? Single-handedly I've made the *Milwaukee Post* one of the most respected papers in the Midwest and the Sunday edition the leading seller in the state. Wonderful! But, Bobbie, I'll let you in on a secret: I go home at night and there's nobody waiting for me and I eat out of paper plates and drink out of paper cups. I was too busy for marriage. I had a purpose. When I said you remind me of myself as a youth, it was not only your initiative that I was thinking of. I thought I could make it on my own too."

"You did make it on your own," Bobbie said quietly.

"And I paid the price. Don't make the same mistake."

Bobbie bristled inwardly. She didn't want anyone feeling sorry for her, especially not her boss. Yet she was touched by the gruff, businesslike editor's concern for her and his admission of vulnerability.

"I know what I'm doing, Cal."

"I hope so." As he got up to go he looked at her oddly with a soft expression. "Obviously I've never had a daughter of my own and I know you've lost your father. So, if things change and wedding bells do toll for you, I'd be honored to walk you down the aisle."

"That's a beautiful sentiment. I'll remember it when I'm old and gray," she tossed off lightly as she tried to swallow the lump in her throat.

"Enough time has been wasted," he barked. "I expect to see a cartoon by this afternoon."

"I'll get right on it, boss." She shrugged off Cal's advice and threw herself totally into her sketch. Hours later the final product, which illustrated the serious water shortage, was timely, witty, and done to perfection.

She realized in the days ahead that she had been avoiding caricaturing the mayor and all his platforms. Every time her mind wandered in that direction, she would unintentionally recall Cal's words and plunge into deep depression. Loneliness became her constant companion.

One evening, having just returned from work, Bobbie was fishing in her purse for the key to the outside door when she heard a kitten meowing at her feet. She stooped to pick it up. "Hello, little cat. Are you hungry?" The tiny yellow kitten purred, as if in response. "Wait here," Bobbie said, putting the kitten down. She ran upstairs for a bowl of milk and a slice of bread. As she watched the voracious way the cat gobbled up what she had brought, she smiled to herself. He purred contentedly in her arms as she stroked him afterward. "Don't think I'm pushy, little cat, but would you like to come and live with me?" she murmured into his velvet ear. When she put him down, he answered her by scampering away, although Bobbie thought he looked back at her with a hint of reluctance in his amber eyes.

He was waiting for her the next evening, and the evening after that he followed her up the stairs but shied away from entering her apartment. He must have been a talker among cats because soon Bobbie was surrounded by a coterie of four cats, who waited for her arrival home each evening in order to serenade her with cries of hunger. She started collecting lunch scraps from people at work and bringing them home with her. She did this religiously and within a week the group of four cats had grown to six. She wished she could swear them to secrecy before this thing got out of hand, but luckily the six remained six. Bobbie thought she looked forward to seeing the cats almost as much as they looked forward to seeing her. She had named the original stray Francis, for what reason she could not say, except that he looked like a Francis, with his screwed-up, homely little face. As Bobbie would get out of her car at night with her soiled and crumpled brown bag, Francis and his cronies would come bounding up to her, causing passersby to stare in amazement. The cats would swarm around her, arching their backs, rubbing up against her legs, and purring happily. A little butterscotch-colored kitten, the runt of the crew, developed the painful habit of climbing up Bobbie's legs. She found that she was going through five pairs of panty hose a week.

At work she began telling Larry and Jerry about the cats on a daily basis. It wasn't long before they insisted on driving home with her to meet them. The cats did Bobbie proud. They were born performers; the more Bobbie and Jerry and Larry would laugh at their antics, the more hilarious they would become. The innocence of their desire for applause was touching.

"Look at Bobbie," Larry said, laughing. "She's crowing like a proud mama!"

"Hmm," Jerry intoned in a professional manner, "this looks like a sublimated maternal instinct. I think you need children, not cats."

"I wish I had a litter box to throw at you," Bobbie blurted out. "All it means is that I like these cats and they like me!"

"I never said this before, but perhaps you made a mistake about Dan," Jerry suggested tentatively. "You used to have a sparkle in your eyes and a special glow in your cheeks. You used to laugh deep belly laughs. Now your laughter comes from your throat—when it comes at all. Sure, you had hassles with Dan, but anything worthwhile is worth fighting for."

"That's quite a speech!" Larry said approvingly. "But you know, he's right, Bobbie. These cats are cute, but they're poor substitutes for what you really want."

"Do you know what I really want?" she asked sharply. "How could you? I don't even know!"

"I think you want the mayor," Jerry said.

Bobbie averted her gaze. "I don't want to talk about the mayor. He's out of my life."

"She's a tough cookie," Larry said, ostensibly to Jerry. "Come on, Bobbie! Jerry and I would like to be ushers at a straight wedding. It would be an interesting change from the usual. Do it for us. Get married!"

"I'll do that at the same time you guys get married—to women!" Bobbie teased.

"I almost made that mistake once, a long time ago,"

180

Jerry admitted ruefully. "It was lucky for both of us that I got out when I did."

"And for me!" Larry added. He looked at Bobbie with a sly grin. "I'm one hundred percent behind Jerry's assessment of your love life—or should I say your lack of one? And you'd better be careful or Jerry and I might tie you up, gag you, and dump you, like a foundling, on the mayor's doorstep."

"He'd know what to do with her!" Jerry laughed raucously.

"And if she's smart, she'd know what to do with him," Larry teased. "He is, after all, the most exciting political figure in the Midwest. You could go far with him."

"Larry!" Bobbie exploded reproachfully. "I'm surprised at you! My interest in the mayor was never motivated by opportunism. And he's exciting in ways other than the political. He's a warm, caring, beautiful man. He's—" Bobbie stopped, embarrassed.

"You still do care about him," Larry said after a long pause.

"You tricked me into saying that!" Bobbie shot back, her hands on her hips.

"So? What are friends for? Go get him, girl, while he's still available."

"The only thing I'm interested in getting is dinner." Bobbie grimaced. "The cats have eaten. Now it's my turn. Would you two like to join me at the corner deli?"

"No, thanks," Larry and Jerry demurred in unison. Jerry, it turned out, had to return to work to develop some pictures and Larry had a previous engagement. Disappointed, for she didn't feel like eating alone, Bobbie thanked them for coming to see the cats.

"I wanted to make sure they weren't a figment of your imagination," Jerry teased.

"Yes," Larry put in. "We wanted to make sure you weren't going off the deep end. You're so sad all the time."

"What's making me sad is you two clucking around me like old mother hens." Bobbie paused and laughed suddenly. "That's not true. You guys are great. I don't know what I'd do without you." As she regarded the earnest, kind faces of her friends she felt choked up with emotion. She was lucky that they were there for her. "It's a lovely evening. The birds are singing, the cats are playing, the air smells fresh, and I'm glad we're friends." She blew them a kiss as they left.

CHAPTER XVIII

Puttering around her small apartment later that evening, Bobbie felt a surge of pent-up energy. That her furniture could have used a dusting and her floors a cleaning did not leave her unawares. That her refrigerator was starting to smell she chose to ignore. She had a choice. She could spend her energy cleaning or she could spend it creating a cartoon. She knew she ought to clean, but she wanted to draw. Fervently hoping that no guests would swoop down on her unexpectedly, she chose to forgo the cleaning and to follow her desires. Taking up a big sketchpad and charcoal pencils, she drew open the ivory-colored macramé draperies that covered the wide windows overlooking the lake. With feet propped up on her handmade black walnut coffee table, she looked out sightlessly, so wrapped up in her thoughts was she. She had intended to do a political cartoon, something about foreign policy or the economy perhaps. All that she could think of was Dan. In her heart of hearts, she knew that her friends were right. She had made a terrible mistake. All the praise in the world that she received from her boss, all the satisfaction she got from her work, the tidy niche she had carved in her corner of the world, could not wash away the tears that flowed freely into her pillow each night. Maybe it had been true that in the grand scheme of things she was unimportant in Dan's life. Maybe she had been only one

183

in a procession of women who danced through his heart. But maybe she had been special. She would never know now, she sighed. Should she have believed his words or the evidence of a heartbroken Sandra? Should the foremost images in her mind be of Dan helping her reel in a bass or of Dan with a faraway look in his eyes, being whisked away in a city limo to more important business? As she thought, her hand, as if of its own accord, sketched. On one page there was a yellow brick road with the tinman on it. Except that he had Bobbie's face, he could have come out of the pages of *The Wizard of Oz*. He was crying rusty tears and the balloon caption that stemmed from his mouth said, "Give me back my heart, please." On another page she had sketched a Valentine heart. It was broken and jagged, pierced by paper clips and a pencil. In disgust Bobbie threw down her pad. She was not accomplishing anything worthwhile. Taking out her vacuum cleaner, she proceeded with her long-overdue housework. In the process of dusting, scrubbing, and polishing she began to feel better. And then her doorbell rang. She wiped her hands on her jeans and opened the door without asking who it was.

"Dan!" Bobbie stepped back, suddenly aware of the old bandanna around her head.

"Hello, Bobbie." Dan smiled down at her, the same devilish smile she remembered.

"Why have you come?"

"The question should be, why haven't I come sooner?" He was silent for a moment, looking at her. "I've come because a friend of yours, Jerry, called me and convinced me that you are in love with me."

"Are you saying that tongue-in-cheek?"

"I'm not. Jerry did call me."

"I never thought of you as a man who would listen to the advice of a stranger."

"Only"—Dan grinned—"when he's seconding my own opinion. Anyway, it was more in the nature of a reminder than a disclosure." Bringing forward the one hand he had been holding behind his back, he proffered a small white bag. "I've brought you something."

"What's this?" Bobbie asked.

"Open it."

Bobbie sniffed at it suspiciously. "It doesn't smell like roses." Opening the package, she giggled. "I don't think I believe this! A liverwurst sandwich!"

"You said you wanted liverwurst and not pâté de foie gras. You had it all along but you didn't know." The smile that stretched across his face melted Bobbie's heart.

"Oh, Dan, I've missed you terribly."

"I missed you too, baby."

"I've been such a fool. I was afraid to love you because I was afraid to lose you. Sandra and Coleman and the feeling that you were married to your career scared me off."

Dan drew her close to him and lifted her face up to his. "Don't let anyone or anything come between us ever again. I don't want us to be like two ships passing in the night. The night is too long and the dawn too magnificent."

"I thought I could make a life by myself," Bobbie continued, feeling it necessary to clear her conscience, "but I've been miserable without you. All this has taught me something: I've learned that without love all the rest of life is empty. Yes, I'm doing well on the paper. *Wisconsin Magazine* even called to say they were considering doing a piece on me—something on the order of 'first successful female cartoonist on big-city newspaper.' I was flattered when I heard but then I realized that the person I most wanted to share the news with was out of my life. Oh,

185

Jerry and Larry toasted me with champagne, but somehow the bubbles seemed a bit flat."

Dan looked down at her thoughtfully. "You've come to the conclusion then that a madcap liberal can find happiness with the staunchest of conservatives?"

"Leave the adjectives out please—*not* madcap! I realize now that politics don't belong in the bedroom. And my heart listens only to my heart. I love you, Dan. I've never said those words to anyone before. It feels strange, but nice."

"Say it again then. I like the way it sounds."

"I love you."

Dan smiled gently. "Is next week too soon?"

"For what?"

"Our wedding. I don't want to take the chance of losing you again."

Bobbie smiled through the tears that started, inexplicably, to roll down her cheeks. "Next week would be perfect."

As she closed her eyes she felt his lips upon hers and knew that from the day of her birth she had been waiting for this moment of harmony and purest bliss. Slipping her arms around his neck, she took a breath. "You do like cats, don't you?"

"Cats are fine. No more talking. Just kiss me again."

LOOK FOR NEXT MONTH'S
CANDLELIGHT ECSTASY ROMANCES™:

When You Want A Little More Than Romance–

Try A Candlelight Ecstasy!

The first novel in the spectacular new
Heiress series

The
English
Heiress
Roberta Gellis

Leonie De Conyers—beautiful, aristocratic, she lived in the
shadow of the guillotine, stripped of everything she held
dear. Roger St. Eyre—an English nobleman, he set out to save
Leonie in a world gone mad.

They would be kidnapped, denounced and brutally sepa-
rated. Driven by passion, they would escape France, return
to England, fulfill their glorious destiny and seize a lofty
dream.

A Dell Book $2.50 (12141-8)

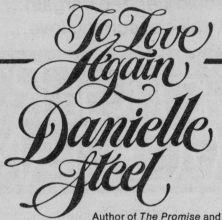